"So, is this good

"I won't leave without seeing you again." Both hands encircled her arms and she thought he was moving closer. The breeze stirred his hair, giving him an even more appealing windblown look.

She lifted her face, lost in the deepening brown of his eyes, watched the way his lips parted slightly as he drew in a breath. And then she saw the troubled brow. His lips touched her bangs, then the tip of her nose.

She closed her eyes, waiting.

Before his lips reached her waiting ones, she moved away. He emitted a sound and stepped back, dropping his hands to his sides.

His hand took hers gently in his and his low, deep voice said, "I will see you after the festival. I'll explain."

What would he explain?

The reason his lips almost touched hers?

Did that require an explanation?

Books by Yvonne Lehman

Love Inspired Heartsong Presents

The Caretaker's Son
Lessons in Love
Seeking Mr. Perfect

YVONNE LEHMAN

is an award-winning, bestselling author of fifty-two novels with more than three million books sold. She is former founder, and director of Blue Ridge Mountains Christian Writers Conference for twenty-five years. Her books have been published by Zondervan, Thomas Nelson, David C. Cook, Guideposts, Barbour, Bethany House, Abingdon, Harlequin Heartsong, and sold in Germany, Norway and Holland. She mentors with the Christian Writers Guild.

Her recent releases are *Hearts that Survive—A Novel of the Titanic* (Abingdon) and a series set in Savannah, Georgia: *The Caretaker's Son, Lessons in Love,* and *Seeking Mr. Perfect.* She blogs along with other authors on ChristiansRead and Novel Rocket. She lives in Black Mountain, in western North Carolina and has traveled in France and Israel.

YVONNE LEHMAN

Seeking
Mr. Perfect

HEARTSONG
PRESENTS

Recycling programs
for this product may
not exist in your area.

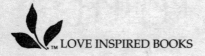 LOVE INSPIRED BOOKS

ISBN-13: 978-0-373-48686-1

SEEKING MR. PERFECT

www.Harlequin.com

Printed in U.S.A.

I know the plans I have for you, says the Lord.
To give you a future and a hope.
—*Jeremiah* 29:11

My writers group for initial brainstorming
and character names, and Lori, whose suggestions
and ideas always intrigue and inspire me.
And thanks to Cindy for our discussions
and accompanying me to Savannah, Georgia.

Chapter 1

Lizzie Marshall watched SweetiePie, the furry white Persian cat, and Mudd, the golden retriever, take turns chasing each other around the yard. Dressed in jeans, a blouse and sandals, Lizzie plopped down on the edge of the porch's top step, knees bent.

She sighed. Obviously she wasn't going to be anybody's sweetie pie, and her prospects were clear as mud. She'd spent all that time on dating websites, and she still hadn't met the man who was right for her. Did that man even exist?

As she watched the dog chase the cat, she wanted to say to the retriever, "Don't bother." He'd never catch the leaping, climbing feline as long as those live oaks and tall magnolias lined the driveway and dotted the spacious green lawn surrounding Aunt B's antebellum mansion. Every time the dog got close, the cat ran up a tree.

Lizzie should take her own advice. Why bother with those dating services anymore? Not that she was desperate or anything, but she rather enjoyed the idea of the clichéd game of boy chases girl until she catches him. The fact was, although she'd liked several guys, she'd never had a really special one. Never one that made her heart pound and her pulse race. At least not since she was about five years old, and that's because she'd been fighting with a boy, at a wedding of all places!

She glanced at the jack-o'-lantern, which had been carved by her recently married friends Annabelle and Symon as a tribute to autumn, and thought it another reminder of things couples did together.

"That fake smile on your round orange face isn't helping," she said to the world's happiest pumpkin. "I'm in charge here for a while, so be careful."

She didn't return Jack's smile.

It wasn't exactly that she was unhappy. Frankly, she was one of the happiest people she knew.

This melancholy would pass. But for the moment she'd bask in her predicament. After all, what's a single girl to do when her friends Megan and Noah Fairfax were on a honeymoon in Hawaii?

Lizzie's gaze wandered to the historic cottage on the other side of the elongated drive, which had been the caretaker's, and was now the home of Annabelle and Symon. She smiled, thinking about Symon, the caretaker's son, who had returned to Savannah as a famous novelist and had won Annabelle's heart.

They'd been married for over a year and were accompanying Aunt B and her French fiancé in Paris. Thinking of Aunt B and Henri made her sigh again, and slump. Even couples in their sixties were falling in love.

Lizzie couldn't be happier for her friends. She'd enjoyed every minute of watching their love stories unfold. It's just that her way of life was changing. She was the single girl in the midst of lovey-dovey married couples, and it was a mite unsettling.

The wind picked up, and she shivered. A cold splat of rain struck her cheek. The forecast predicted a storm, even the promise of a deluge. Gray cloud pillows rolled across the darkening sky.

Rising, she called for the animals. Mudd ambled toward her, expecting a treat for obedience. SweetiePie ignored her. She'd come at her own discretion. Lizzie picked up Jack. "Better get you inside before you're blown away and splattered against those oaks and magnolias. After all, you were carved with love."

At the rumble of thunder, SweetiePie decided to skitter past her as she was propping open the screen door with her backside and wrestling with fifteen pounds of pumpkin. Tail wagging, a panting Mudd blocked the way in front of her as if he thought she kept treats inside Smiling Jack.

"Nothing in here for you, Mudd."

She scooted the dog inside. There! Everyone safe and dry. She peered out the kitchen window and viewed Spanish moss dripping with tears, which poured from the crying clouds.

This sadness was not her way.

Always…always before, she'd made funnies about her plight. She'd joked. She'd self-denigrated. But nobody was here to see her now. No one to convince that all was well, and she'd simply try another date from Christian Singles. She did not feel like praying anymore…for Mr. Perfect.

The Lord either didn't hear her, didn't care or wanted her to forever be a spinster. Okay, so her mid-twenties wasn't technically old enough to be called a spinster, but all her friends were getting married and she'd been left behind. Walking through the dim hallway, Lizzie was just facing the truth.

There was only one thing to do. After checking the house to make sure all doors were shut and windows closed, she stood in her upstairs bedroom. Not hers really.

She'd moved in with Aunt B when Megan had decided to turn her house, where Lizzie, Megan and Annabelle had lived while in college, into a B and B. Megan would live in Noah's house after their honeymoon.

Ever since Lizzie's mother had read *Cinderella, Snow White* and *Sleeping Beauty* to her as a child, Lizzie had dreamed of a prince charming on a white steed showing up. Well, she was twenty-five years old and it was about time she faced reality.

Her efforts of praying for a special someone hadn't brought results. Oh, they brought guys from the dating service, but they were never Mr. Perfect, at least not for her. Or maybe she was Miss Imperfect.

As she thought about it, she realized she'd prayed about a special guy and then set about trying to find one. Maybe that wasn't the way to do it.

She fell on her knees beside the bed, like she'd done in her own home, by her own bed, when she was a child.

Back then, she'd prayed for a handsome prince who would come and take her away to live happily ever after.

With folded hands, bowed head and closed eyes, she prayed.

Lord,
Maybe I've been wrong in trying to find Mr. Perfect all these years. I've exhausted the heap of men on the Christian dating services. None were right. Or I was wrong. So I'm giving up. I'm letting go. If you want me to have a special guy, then bring him to me. I won't go hunting anymore. I won't look for him around every corner.

If for some strange reason I'm to remain single, I'm accepting that. If you have a plan for my life other than what I'm doing now, let me know. From now on, I'm not looking for, or expecting, a man.

Opening her eyes, she started to get up, then thought better of it. She had to do this all the way. She sighed and closed her eyes again.

> *In case you doubt my sincerity, I won't keep the date*
> *that's set up for tonight. I won't go through with it.*
> *My struggle is over.*
> *Love,*
> *I mean, Amen.*

She rose from her kneeling position. Unfortunately she didn't feel any better. In fact, her knees felt tight and her calves tingly. But one's faith and commitment didn't depend on feelings, so she'd been told.

And everything wasn't abundant joy all the time.

Maybe when she was sixty-three, she'd be like Aunt B, and—

Oops! No.

No more.

How odd. Instead of wondering if the date tonight was Mr. Perfect, she would simply break the date.

The rain pounded the roof and splattered the windows, as if saying she'd washed those men right out of her hair. Well, if she'd *had* any men.

Her date was supposed to meet her at the Pirate's Cave restaurant. The most piratelike she had intended to be this evening was wearing a white full-sleeved shirt over jeans and a skull-and-crossbones-printed bandanna around her neck. But since she was breaking her date, she might as well dress in full pirate regalia.

Whatever. She had a six o'clock date to break. She was forever done with trying to find Mr. Perfect.

Well, that was a baby step, wasn't it?

The loud rumble of thunder sounded like a yes.

* * *

The TV weather report stated the roads were already flooded. If she and her brother hadn't owned Pirate's Cave, she'd quit her waitressing job rather than chance the storm. As the lights in the house flickered, she decided she'd be better off with Paul than alone in this big house with a dog, a cat and Smiling Jack.

Paul would never leave the restaurant as long as a customer could possibly arrive. He'd consider it a safe place for anyone stranded, too. But no self-respecting tourist would come out in this storm. That thought made Lizzie feel better. If her date arrived at the restaurant, it meant he was a non-self-respecting person so she wouldn't want him anyway.

She donned her hooded rain poncho and learned the meaning of braving the elements and ran to her car. A few minutes later she reached the cobbled stones of River Street, and saw several cars in front of shops, including one at the Pirate House. In her email, she'd instructed her date not to mistake that restaurant for the Pirate's Cave.

Seeing a car already in front of the Cave made her heart lurch. She parked a few feet behind it, dreading what she had to do. However, she could give that car a little shove, causing it to float down the street. She'd run in the restaurant and say, "Hey, your car's getting away. Better go get it."

No, she couldn't do that. He might drown or break his neck, and that would be her fault. She doubted that's the way God wanted her to break a date.

Not intending to wade through the rushing tide along the curb, she slid out the passenger side, and stepped onto the street. The wind threatened to blow her in another direction but she managed to open the front door of the Cave, which activated the pirate's ship foghorn—fitting on an evening like this.

Fighting against the wind, she shoved the door closed. A quick glance around revealed no customers. She skulked toward the dining room quietly, not wanting her booted heels to sound on the wooden planks. She peered in. Seeing only a middle-aged couple at a table, she breathed a sigh of relief and trekked back across the planks. Paul came from the kitchen. Shucking out of her poncho, she said the obvious. "Surely my date won't come."

"If he does, I can already assess him," Paul said. "He's too desperate. Anyone who'd risk their life… Oops, sorry. You did." He grinned. "I thought of calling and telling you not to come. But I knew neither rain, sleet, snow nor hail could keep you away from a date."

"I'm going to break the date." She hung her poncho on a hook on the side wall, then faced him and lifted her chin. "I've quit trying to find a special someone."

She knew a skeptical look and a wry grin when she saw them. "I mean it." She lifted her right hand in a vow position.

His eyebrows rose.

"Really." Racing through her mind were the college guys she'd gone out with, the models she'd met through Annabelle's connections, out-of-state tourists she'd scrutinized when taking Megan's historic tours and the past few years of dating guys from Christian Singles services. Just thinking of it made her tired. "No more." She perched on a stool at the countertop and traced her finger along the pirate treasure map embedded in the granite.

Paul spoke low, garnering her attention. "Are you telling me that my days of scrutinizing, eavesdropping, searching the internet and watching for anything unsuitable in all those guys are over?" Propping his forearms on the countertop, he shook his head of auburn curls. "What will we do with our free time? Your dating escapades took up nine-tenths of it." Leaning back, he grimaced. "And my guest room? My interrogation of your prospects?"

Guilt made her reach out and lay her hand on his. Too often she took him for granted. "I guess you don't have time to think about yourself, with your looking out for me and spending so much time here at the Cave."

He laughed. "Believe me, knowing you and Annabelle and Megan gives me a pretty clear idea of what I want in a woman." He looked at her with affection. "But my life is busy, and I'm not complaining."

Did he mean that knowing them made him want to stay single?

She didn't want to know. Her confidence was low enough.

"All I've wanted was a special someone," Lizzie said, as if he hadn't heard this before. "Now that Annabelle and Megan are married, I'm feeling sort of left out." She shrugged. "Maybe I'll be a waitress for the rest of my life."

"You're the best, sis. But you can do anything you want."

Her glance moved to the dining room where Cheryl, dressed in her pirate outfit, refilled the couple's tea glasses and talked with them.

Lizzie returned her attention to Paul when he said, "You're really serious about this?"

She nodded. "I promised God I'd break the date tonight. And I won't contact the dating services again. If God wants me to have a man, he will have to bring him to me."

A car door slammed. Lizzie heard thunder either from the heavens or from her insides. She glanced at the treasure map clock. Two minutes 'til six. Her date would come out in this weather? He must be desperate. The second hand kept moving. She turned on the stool as the foghorn sounded and the wind propelled a figure inside the open door.

He wore a long black trench coat like a swashbuckler

in a romance novel. Laughing lightly, he closed the black umbrella and placed it in the urn by the door. A head of dark wet hair surrounded the most appealing face she'd ever seen, and she'd seen many.

"Arrrgh," she said. The word just slipped out. More easily than she slipped from the stool. This time "arrrgh" was not the greeting she used when pretending to be a pirate for the tourists who came in.

This *arrrgh* was definitely a moan, a groan of the total mess she'd made of her life. She always spoke or acted too quickly, and this time she'd done it big-time. Made a promise to God right before a man who had to be Mr. Perfect walked through the door and stood staring at her—with a smile on his full wide lips in a face that begged to be touched.

Lizzie couldn't smile. If she tried, she'd look like orange-faced Jack.

She could only stare. He must feel it, too. That unexplainable—

Then he spoke. A golden, musical voice matching the glint in his expressive dark eyes. Eyes lined by long dark lashes a girl would die for. He said something that sounded as if he didn't know Savannah had a woman like her.

She heard Paul say, "It's unusual—the edge of a hurricane. But it's passing through. Should be gone in a few hours."

Oh, Mr. Tall Dark and Handsome must have said *storm* instead of *woman*. Her shining knight on a white horse was dressed in black. That must mean he was a temptation sent from God…or somewhere…to test her.

Paul said something about going into the dining room to speak to the couple who was getting ready to leave. Lizzie glanced at her brother with pleading eyes, but he grinned and lifted his eyebrows as if to say she was on her own. That returned her to semireality. She'd better hurry and set the man in black straight.

"I'm so sorry." She needed to do this quickly before she reneged on her promise to God. She could only admire a man who would come out in this deluge and risk his life just to meet her. "I have to break our date. This is a recent decision. I wasn't able to let you know ahead of time. I'm through with dating. If you want to order something from the menu, that's all I can offer."

His glance shifted to the front windows. He must be totally shocked into silence. Maybe he had felt that connection and was now...devastated?

What had she done?

Could she tell God she was just kidding? Well, he knew her heart. She hadn't been kidding. And now she'd ruined her chances of ever being happy.

The answer to her prayer was clear. The Lord wanted her to suffer in spinsterhood forever.

She hadn't noticed Cheryl enter the room. The waitress handed Lizzie a menu, and she hardly glanced at it. Her focus was on the little furrow of concern that worried the dreamboat's brow.

She stepped back because his aura was invading her space. "If you want the Pirate Tour, fine." She was trying to get into the pirate mode, but didn't seem to be out of the dating mode just yet. "But don't think I'm playing hard to get, because I'm not. I'm impossible to get because I don't intend to be gotten. I'm getting on with my life, my way..."

His dark, thick eyelashes shaded eyes that weren't meeting hers. He appeared contemplative, probably trying to absorb his disappointment. His hand moved to the wet wavy hair falling softly over his forehead. He pushed it back. She could have done that for him. Would have liked to. But, she was grasping a menu.

She thought she noticed a slight grimace on his face, but his eyes held a trace of merriment when he gazed into hers again. Yes, she'd been right. He was good-natured.

Lizzie looked up at him. The dating service had said he was new in town. His profile didn't contain a picture, but it described him as tall, dark and handsome. Apparently the dating service people didn't read romance novels, or lacked in creative description. He was Mr. Wonderful. He seemed to have difficulty undoing the top fastener of his trench coat. Perhaps his shaking hand indicated that he sensed her emotions, and possibly felt the same way.

Her phone vibrated against her leg, and she retrieved it from her pocket. She didn't recognize the number, and she turned from the man still fumbling with his buttons.

"Hello?"

She could hardly believe what the caller was saying. Her date was apologizing, saying the weather was too rough and his electricity was off. She wished she could say the same. Her date, that she'd vowed not to keep, was on the line. So Mr. Wonderful who just blew in was the one meant for her.

She could barely contain her joy. God didn't want her to be single after all. At the same time she was breaking the date, she was meeting the one meant for her.

Lizzie quickly told the date all was fine. No, not to call again. Other things had come up. She turned around to face her man.

His coat opened. Her eyes widened and her jaw dropped, and she wished there was an opening in the planks beneath her boots so she could fall through it. She felt sure her heart had.

She must look a sight because surely her red hair, green eyes and brown freckles clashed with her skin, which was turning blue because she wasn't breathing.

He shucked out of his trench coat and laid it on the back of the booth. His hands moved to his waist and soft black material fell to his ankles as he said, "Tucked my skirt in so it wouldn't get wet."

Chapter 2

Lizzie felt light-headed. She choked, coughed and managed to clear her throat enough to rasp, "Water" and hold her hand out toward him.

"No, thanks. I'd rather have coffee."

Cheryl apparently had noticed her distress and was already on the way with a glass. Lizzie took it and drank. She breathed. Hyperventilated, really.

"I'll hang this up for you," Cheryl said to the man, and took his coat. He slid into the booth. Cheryl brought water for him and tapped the menu so Lizzie laid it in front of him. Unable to speak, she galumphed to the dining room.

Paul hurried to her. "Sis, what's wrong?"

Still too shocked to speak, she made a face and gestured with her head toward the man behind her. Her brother looked back at her questioningly. She grazed her index finger across her neck.

Paul peered into the front room. "He's a flasher and you want me to cut his throat?"

Lizzie found somebody's voice and squeaked out, "He's wearing one of those little white dumaflaches."

"I think it's called a clerical collar."

"Whatever." She lifted her hands. "I insulted him. Told him I didn't want a man. And then he shows his…" She took another breath. "His collar."

Paul shrugged. "At least he knows where you stand. And he's still there, so maybe he's glad you don't want him since he's a member of the clergy."

"Should I ask his forgiveness?"

Paul scrunched his face. "Not unless you do want him."

She hit him and he laughed, heading for the kitchen.

Lizzie returned to the booth and studied the man's profile. What were the words? *Statuesque? Chiseled?* Whatever…he looked great. She had an apology to make.

"Sir." Maybe that would help. "I thought you were something else. I mean someone else. Well, not anyone I know. I mean, you're not from the dating service, are you?"

He shook his head. "Could I have a cup of coffee?"

"Coffee?" she repeated as if the word were foreign to her.

His glance shifted again and settled on the window, which was being beaten by the rain and wind. He probably wondered which was safer, outside in the storm, or inside with a pirate who'd lost her mind.

Lizzie couldn't find her voice. It often disappeared when she was trying to find words to ease the tension. Fortunately, Cheryl was nearby and said, "I'll get the coffee."

"With cream," he said to Cheryl, then looked at Lizzie. "I've heard worse." She thought she saw the light dancing in his eyes. "Before coming here, I counseled a fellow who made me promise confidentiality, then confessed to committing atrocious crimes." He cleared his throat and gave a light chuckle. "You have a lovely mouth, but I'm still undecided about the tonsils."

She closed her lips and hinged her jaw back in place. Staring out the windows, obscured by blowing rain, she asked, "Think he followed you?"

"No, he has to pick up someone from the airport."

She cautioned her jaw to remain in place and her tonsils hidden.

"I have a confession to make, too." He reached down and pinched the black material. "This isn't a skirt. It's a clerical robe." He smiled.

Seemed logical, considering the clerical collar.

Still rather discombobulated, she pulled at the sleeve of her shirt. "This isn't exactly my everyday attire." Oh, dear, his probably was. Well, so was hers in a way.

"You work here?"

She thought of firing herself, but replied, "Usually," as Cheryl appeared with his coffee and cream.

"You want anything?" Cheryl asked her.

"I'll just hang on to my water. Thanks." She glanced at the man. "You want to look at the menu?"

"In a moment." He poured cream into his coffee and stirred. Laying the spoon aside, he glanced around the room. "Is this the place Sy DeBerry used as the setting for his latest book?" He picked up his cup and sipped the coffee.

"Yes. Symon was intrigued by the history of the Cave." She was glad to think of something other than her embarrassment or insulting him by saying she couldn't date him. "And with the pirate stories I had told him."

"Ah." He set down his cup. "Like the Red Lady in his book?"

Relaxing somewhat, she smiled, thinking of the tale. "That's the one I told him the first time he came in here with my friend Annabelle. She and Symon are married now."

The man had an expressive face. His eyes showed interest. In fact they danced with it, as if he'd found gold. "And what did you tell him about the Red Lady?"

Now she wished she'd worn the Red Lady costume. She felt much more at ease in a pirate's skin than her own. "Just a minute." She set her glass on the table, then marched over to the wall near the coat hooks and retrieved a black pirate's hat. Returning, she tucked her long ponytail and thick bangs underneath it and pulled the hat farther down her forehead. Now, she felt in character.

"I'm Veronica, and I'm from the sixteenth century. I board the ships as an entertainer or singer." She began exaggerating. "Yo, ho, ho and a bottle of…" She stopped and laughed. "A bottle of water, of course."

Good. His laugh meant his sense of humor was intact, so she continued.

"Underneath my attractive attire, which makes me look like a rather plump, innocent lady, I'm wearing a shirt, pants and weapons. At the first opportunity, I remove my disguise and… Oops."

She didn't have the sword.

Seeing her predicament, Cheryl went to the wall and retrieved it for her. Lizzie took it and swung. "I kill everyone aboard. Then the ship is mine and I sail out to sea." With a flourish, she bowed.

"Ah, I love it," he said, leaning back against the corner of the booth. "I could listen to stories like that all evening." He motioned to the seat across from him and she perched on the end of it. "Too bad you don't have a way to say you're not available other than that tirade you were on."

She nodded. "I was nervous about telling the guy. It's so foreign to what I usually do." She laughed, uncomfortable. She stared at the black-and-white material at his neck. "I don't think I could wear a collar. Somebody might just hook a leash on it and lead me around."

He chuckled and kept looking at her with those mis-

chievous eyes. He had really nice eyes. Like warm chocolate. More like hot fudge, kind of delicious…if he wasn't a
clergyman. She was getting close to blasphemy. "Maybe I
should paint a scarlet letter on my forehead."

He stared back, eyes wide. "Oh, no!" She tried to explain. "That's the only thing I could think of at the moment.
I'm not a scarlet woman. I can't even find a decent—"

He had the grace, probably from God, to lift a hand
and smile. Oh, what a face. "I can understand you would
be a temptation. With that scarlet hair of yours. And your
freckles are absolutely adorable on your lovely face. Green
eyes? How rare. I mean, they're like jewels."

Lizzie couldn't blink. Her eyes felt like they had turned
to stone.

The man's face became serious. "Would you like to
join me for dinner and tell me all about your troubles?"

She knew she could not sit there and look at that face
and into those eyes. He was too distracting.

A sudden rattling of the windows drew his attention. His
full lips tightened as he looked out the window. She knew
she shouldn't be staring at his mouth, but she couldn't help
it. God was probably going to strike her dead. She *did* hear
a rumble of thunder.

He faced her again. "Maybe after dinner you could take
me on the pirate tour."

"I can do that," she said. "Are you ready to order? No
wine, huh?"

He smiled and said soberly, "I think I can wait for the
Eucharist."

"Who? Oh. Like…the Lord's Supper?"

He pointed a finger at her as if she got it. "For now, I'd
like…my supper."

"Yes, um, should I call you 'sir'?"

His eyebrows lifted but his gaze went to the menu.

Lizzie scooted out of the booth seat as Paul walked out

from the kitchen. "Sorry," he said. "No more dinners tonight. The wind has picked up and there are some fallen trees. Electricity is out in some places and I'm afraid we'll lose power in the middle of cooking someone's meal." He focused on the clergyman. "Come back tomorrow evening, and nature permitting, dinner's on the house."

"Thanks," he said, and turned his attention to Lizzie again. "One more thing." A tiny groove appeared between those expressive brows. "I heard DeBerry's first book is being made into a movie. Maybe they'll film some of it here."

She shook her head. "That deal fell through."

"Oh? That's too bad." He raised his cup and drained it. "Good coffee."

He slid out of the booth and lifted his skirt...no, robe. Then reached into the pocket of his jeans. Jeans? Well, what did she think he'd wear?

"On the house," she said. "The least I can do for telling a clergyman I can't date him."

He laughed a wonderful deep chuckle.

Cheryl brought over his trench coat, and he shrugged into it. "Well, Veronica. I hope to see you tomorrow."

"It's a—" She'd started to say date. "Plan."

He bent toward her, as if bowing, reminding her of Aunt B's Parisian fiancé. He didn't kiss her hand, however, and she said, "I'll reserve a table, um, Pastor...?"

"For now, Veronica, just think of me as Rev. Dr. Preston Bartholomew."

He shouldn't have told her to think of him. She was already thinking of hitting herself in the head with a hammer so she wouldn't.

When he opened the door, the wind blew the pirate hat from her head. But she didn't move. The last thing she saw as he forcefully pulled the door closed and disappeared was the amusement in his dark eyes.

If the electricity were to go off, it wouldn't matter. The warmth coursing through her from just looking at the man was enough to power the entire Cave.

He fit her first requirement. He was a man of faith. But this was overdoing it a bit. She wondered if his church allowed him to marry.

Chapter 3

Zachary Grant didn't bother opening the umbrella as he left the Cave lest it make a Mary Poppins out of him. A very wet one, that is. He did try to keep the hem of his clerical robes out of the water, though, so the wardrobe people wouldn't get on his case. He was wearing the costume from his most recent acting job, and he hoped it would dry by morning. He smiled. The beautiful redhead had believed he was a pastor. Maybe he was a good actor.

His shiny black shoes sloshed over the brick sidewalk. Hanging on to the car so he wouldn't blow away, he stretched over the curb, avoiding the huge puddles, and carefully made his way into the driver's seat. Seeing only a few cars parked along the street, he tried a U-turn that almost turned into an O-turn, but straightened the car out and hoped his memory served him right because his eyes weren't doing so well. Thanks to the storm, he could barely see the road.

He glanced out the passenger-side window at the Savannah River—an impressionistic picture of yellow-white lights on the tips of churning wind-whipped water. He hoped the river posed no flooding problem and would empty its excess into the Atlantic Ocean.

The street demanded his focus for the slow journey. The setting reminded him of the first time he had sat in his car as a teenager while giant brushes and huge hoses dumped a deluge on him at the local car wash. Hoping for air had been like hoping to breathe under water. If he could manage to open the door to escape, he'd be brushed and beaten to a pulp. The air inside the car grew staler. His heart beat faster. His eyes widened. After what had seemed like two hours, a blinking light had finally appeared with the words You're Finished.

That's what he'd thought.

It had taken him a while to calm down, lower his heart rate and steady his hand enough to shift the car into Drive and pull away as a wiser teen in a clean car.

Now, Zachary Grant laughed.

So…the heavens decided to have a world-wash tonight. Nothing to fear.

"Yo, ho, ho and shiver me timbers," he sang in the best pirate voice he could manage under the circumstances. The windshield wipers sounded like drums and the sloshy churning tires provided accompaniment. The wildly swinging traffic lights signaled "Lights, camera, action!" Just like a movie set.

He laughed, driving in the center of the street to avoid the rushing streams along the sides of the curbs. He leaned over the steering wheel as if that would improve visibility. Despite the weather, he smiled. Any other time he might have considered such a scene one out of *Twilight Zone*.

But not tonight. He wasn't concerned about maneuvering the car along the few blocks to Jones Street. He turned off the brick road and onto the drive leading to the parking places at the back of the B and B, as close as he could get to the side entry. Feeling like Gene Kelly, he considered dancing in the rain. However, he trekked across the patio and breathed easier upon reaching steps partially protected by a wall and a roof.

He climbed to the second floor, entered and squished down the hallway. He heard the muted sound of a TV from behind the closed door of a middle-aged couple he'd met at breakfast.

Cliff appeared at his open door and propped his arm against the casing. "Your skirt's wet."

"Funny."

"I figured you'd be washed away by now."

"Tonight I could just about walk on water." He laughed at the lift of Cliff's eyebrows. Zach pulled aside the trench coat and pointed to the collar. "Being Rev. Bartholomew has its advantages."

At the rumble of thunder, Cliff cast a glance toward the ceiling. "Beware."

Zach chuckled. "The pirate lady at that restaurant is none other than a friend of Sy DeBerry's wife."

Cliff was not impressed. "Logical, isn't it, since DeBerry credits that restaurant as the inspiration for writing *The Pirate's Treasure*." He shrugged. "And depends on what you mean by friend. Personal or social media."

Zach felt as if more than just his clothes were dampened, thinking of his many friends and media followers he didn't know and likely never would.

"Just trying to throw in a little reality," Cliff said. "You gotta dream, but sorry to say, your production company is small potatoes compared to the one that optioned DeBerry's book."

Zach grimaced at the feel of his feet in his soaked socks. Any other time Cliff might be throwing a wet blanket of reality on his hopes, but not tonight. His intent had been to become familiar with that restaurant in case he might be considered to play a part in the film adaptation of DeBerry's novel.

But the pirate lady likely had no idea what she'd revealed. The possibilities instantly became bigger. His dream of producing a major movie seemed to have fallen into his hands.

With the film festival starting in a few days, every major studio that knew the deal had fallen through with DeBerry's book would be on the novelist's doorstep. Instead, Zach Grant was on his doorstep so to speak, and likely because of a slip of the tongue from that girl who wasn't going to date anymore. He didn't want to chance his own slip of the tongue about what he had found out tonight. Not even with Cliff.

He sniffed. "You have food in there?"

Cliff shook his head. "That's dinner you smell. Oh, man, that woman can cook."

"Isn't this place breakfast only?"

"She said she wasn't going home in this storm so she cooked dinner. It was free, too."

"I'll check it out." He paused. "Aren't you supposed to be at the airport?"

Cliff lifted his shoulders. "Flight's delayed." He snorted. "Surprise, surprise. Anyway, I'm packed and ready to pick up Marlene and go to the hotel. I still don't get why they don't allow unmarried couples to stay here together."

Zach shrugged. "Conservative South."

"Well, thanks for getting me in here tonight. I'd hate to drive to the hotel in this."

"No problem. I'll see you at the festival."

"Right." Cliff backed up and closed his door.

Zach's shoes squeaked their way to his suite. After a quick shower and changing into jeans and a knit shirt, he descended the stairs, marched through the hallway and into the kitchen. The dishwasher was humming and so was the cook. She glanced over her shoulder at him.

He figured he looked as hungry as he felt.

She turned toward him, put her hands on her hips and questioned him with her big brown eyes. "You looking for something?" she said in a sassy way.

Although he'd spent only his early years in the South, other than a few visits, he knew there were some people you didn't mess with, and she'd be one of them. He tried his best pitiful look. "I missed dinner."

"I noticed," she said. "When your Hollywood friend said you didn't have sense enough to come in out of the rain, I 'spected you had raw fish or duck for your supper."

He thought she'd paraphrased Cliff's remark. Zach knew Cliff well—his words would have been a little harsher than that! Judging by the inflection in her tone she didn't care much for Hollywood types.

Trying not to be intimidated, but having known women like her could rule anybody's household, he held on to the back of a chair and attempted drawling a few words. "I happen to know there's never a lack of good Southern cooking. Maybe there's a biscuit and that gravy left over from breakfast?"

She huffed. "If you know anything about the South you know we don't let nobody go hungry and there's always something left over."

"Any…Southern fried chicken?"

"No," she said, "I went up north to cook it." She rolled her eyes, then stepped over to the refrigerator and took out a foil-covered platter. "Just wrapped this up so it's still warm. But I can heat it up."

He shook his head. "No, ma'am. I can't wait that long."

"Well, you pour your own coffee, and I'll see what else I can whip up for you." She set the platter on the table.

He reached toward it, and she jerked it away, pointing

to the sink. "You wash your hands. Then we'll have the blessing."

Zach did as he was told, wondering if she'd inspect his fingernails. He returned to the table, and folded his hands in front of him, afraid if he touched the chair she might make him wash again. She'd said a blessing before their breakfast that morning so when she looked at him he bowed his head, closed his eyes and remained silent.

"Precious Lord, help this boy in the ways he needs. And bless this food to his nourishment. Amen."

He stepped over to the coffeepot.

"I'm supposed to ask this," she said. "Is everything meeting your expectations?"

"More than I can say. The filming went smoothly despite the roaring elements."

She grunted. "I'm talking about here at the B and B."

He hadn't given it a lot of thought. Due to the flight delay, he and Cliff had gotten in after midnight. He'd been pleasantly surprised that he had a sitting room attached to his bedroom and a private bath. Saw nothing to complain about.

"The soap," he said. "It lathers like crazy. What kind is that?" Uh-oh, he thought he left some suds in the sink.

He set his coffee on the table as she piled a feast onto a plate and stuck it in the microwave. She set a little creamer on the table. He sat and poured a little in his coffee while she opened a drawer and brought out silverware. "This is an unofficial supper so you can use a paper napkin."

He lifted the foil covering on the chicken platter. "From the looks and smell of this, I'll probably just lick my fingers."

Her hands went to her hips. "Not in my kitchen you won't. Now eat before that chicken gets cold."

He didn't have to be told twice.

"And it's not the soap," she said. "It's the water."

"The water?"

She nodded. "Soft water. That's what makes the soap lather," referring to the remark he'd made, but had forgotten. "Reminds me of living water."

"Well, it's alive out there tonight."

He thought she rolled her eyes again, but the microwave tinged so she got his plate and set it on the table. "I 'spect you're here for the film festival."

"That I am. You go to it?"

Her eyebrows lifted. "I've had my fill of Hollywood movies."

He laughed lightly. "There are some good ones. I guess you know Sy DeBerry."

She gave him a look. "I reckon we Savannah people know him better than you Hollywood people. He lives here."

"Yes, I know. And I'm not Hollywood. I'm Malibu." Afraid she might take his food away, he tried to soften her. "I lived in Savannah until I was twelve."

"That right?"

"That's right. My parents lived near here. The Grants. That's why I jumped at the chance to stay here. Just recently learned this was turned into a B and B." He chomped into the chicken. Yes, he'd lick his fingers even if he had to duck under the table to do it. "I've walked along Jones Street many times. Had a friend who lived around the corner."

"It's only been a B and B a few months." She turned. "You have to be somebody or know somebody to stay here. Who do you know?"

She knew how to put a person in his place. "My dad keeps up with what's going on in Savannah. Has friends here that he visits. He's the one who told me DeBerry lives here. I'd sure like to meet him."

She stared at him. "Is that right?"

The question sounded as if she was saying fat chance. "You read his pirate book?" he asked.

"Mmm-hmm," she hummed.

"What did you think of it?"

"Well, I think instead of the detectives searching for that horrible killer, Symon should have made the murderer eat like you're doing and let him choke on a chicken bone."

Zach practically choked on the bite of food in his mouth. He coughed several times, then gulped down some coffee. "You trying to kill me?"

"You're doing all right by yourself."

Man, she reminded him of the cook and housekeeper his family had years ago. "May I ask your name?"

"Willamina."

"Mine's Zach."

"I know," she said blandly. "And you're in the Magnolia Room. You've had a lot of small acting parts in movies, including playing the part of a pastor in a movie that's being filmed at the historic church. Your daddy made it big in movies. And you started your own production company a couple years ago."

He swallowed his mashed potatoes. "Do you know that because you're a fan?" He laughed at that, so she wouldn't have to insult him. "Or you knew my parents, or did you overhear the conversation in the dining room this morning?"

"I don't know that I've seen you in a movie," she said. "We screen the guests who come here. Don't want any surprises."

"Thanks," he said, and dug into the food again. From his experience in the movie industry, he knew things happened because of who you knew.

He also knew you struck while the iron was hot. The early bird gets the worm. Clichés, but they fit. An even more fitting expression might be that Zach Grant had met a pirate lady and that was a feather in his cap.

Or…a skull and crossbones on his hat.

Better yet…a parrot on his shoulder.

If he could impress DeBerry, or even make personal contact with him, Zach could be on his way to the big time. Pretty good for a fellow in his early thirties. When he had been listening to the redheaded, green-eyed, freckled-nosed, pirate lady, he'd kept his mind on being Rev. Bartholomew and not a man admiring an intriguing woman. He worked with beauties all the time, but right now he was working on a career. Nothing wrong with Rev. Bartholomew returning to that restaurant and learning how he might impress DeBerry with his knowledge and ideas, when and if, he met him.

Yes, wearing a clerical collar had its benefits.

The heavens rumbled and the house shook. Maybe that was simply nature applauding his acting tonight.

Chapter 4

Lizzie awoke with a start, and had to blink several times to make sense of her surroundings. Her eyes found the light peeking around the windows and then she remembered she wasn't in her own room. But where were the animals? And what was that aroma?

Slowly, the meaning began to dawn on her like the morning sun pushing its glow against the blinds. She'd slept in Aunt B's bedroom downstairs. Slept after midnight that is, after the howling wind turned to whispers. She hadn't wanted to chance being upstairs in case the edge of the hurricane took off the top of the house.

Paul had insisted upon making sure she got to the house all right last night and *she* had insisted he stay instead of driving out to Tybee Island. He slept in the downstairs guest room, and now that she was beginning to awaken, she knew the aroma was a result of him making breakfast.

Slipping out of bed and into her slippers, she laughed, remembering how close SweetiePie had cuddled to her last night instead of roaming the house. Symon's golden retriever eyed her fearfully from beneath the bed. Mudd usually slept on the floor beside her bed, but last night had hidden underneath it until the stormy tumult had ceased. Lizzie wondered if the dog remembered the hurricane, when he had been trapped by debris. She walked out of her room and down the hall, Mudd following at her heels.

"You know how to wake a girl," Lizzie said, walking into the kitchen and heading for the coffeepot.

Paul scooted the spatula beneath a hash brown and flipped it. The scent of potato and onion along with whatever spices or herbs he might have used whetted her appetite. "Nothing fancy," he said. "Don't want to do too much damage to Aunt B's kitchen."

"Willamina's kitchen, you mean." Lizzie took a cup from the cupboard. "The house is Aunt B's. The kitchen is Willamina's." She laughed and poured her coffee. She walked over to the table and sat.

Paul put the hash browns on plates, cooked sunny-side up eggs, then brought their breakfast to the table. He set the plates on the chargers. "No time for biscuits," he told her as he popped bread into the toaster. "You want to pray?"

She glanced at the toaster. "You want a short one, I guess."

He laughed and stepped over to grasp the chair back. "Well, yes. You have to stop when the toaster flips the bread up."

She thanked God for the safety of the night, the care her wonderful brother gave her and the scrumptious breakfast. Paul's cooking was better than a frozen waffle in the toaster.

"Amen."

She and her brother loved each other. Needed each other. She hadn't found it easy to move out of the house and room with Annabelle and Megan during her college years. But she'd known it was best, and more convenient, than driving in each day from Tybee Island.

"Have there been any reports about damage on Tybee?" she asked as he brought the toast and butter to the table.

"Minor wind damage." He buttered his toast. "I'll need to get out there and make sure the house is okay, get myself cleaned up and be at the Cave before the lunch crowd comes in."

Lizzie savored the delectable hashbrowns. "Cheryl could open up, you know. And the cooks know what to do."

His gaze was level. "I make up my own mind."

She nodded. She tried not to look at the animals at her feet, but couldn't help herself. SweetiePie and Mudd stared up at her, both in sitting positions. Her big shining blue eyes and his round brown ones pleaded pitifully. Unable to resist, she tore off a few bites of toast crust, making sure there was a taste of butter on it. She tossed it to the animals. They leaped and gobbled it up.

"You're not supposed to do that," Paul reprimanded.

"I know."

She knew, too, that she wasn't supposed to think about the pastor from last night—the most appealing man she'd seen in a long time, if ever. And it wasn't just his looks. She'd thought Symon and Noah were particularly good-looking, but she'd never experienced that certain spark. She'd even talked about the feeling to her friends. She'd recognized it between Annabelle and Symon, Megan and Noah, Aunt B and Henri. She should not feel that spark for a clergyman, particularly one whose church was so formal that he needed to wear a robe and collar, even out in public. If anybody in the world wasn't cut out to be a pastor's wife, it was her. She was far too free-spirited and outspoken. She was probably just reacting to the fact that he was forbidden. Plus, she'd made that vow. Must be her baser nature acting up.

She had to lecture herself again that afternoon after Paul called from the Cave.

"Your pastor called," he said.

Oh, dear. She had hoped he wouldn't come. Now disappointment swept through her at that likelihood. "Can he not come?"

"He made an appointment for six o'clock and asked if Veronica, the pirate lady could give him a tour."

"Did you tell him that whoever is available gives the tours?"

"I said we aim to please. Veronica would be delighted."

"How can someone as nice as you be so vindictive?"

"No reason not to accommodate." He paused. "Unless you have a reason not to trust him."

"It's not him I don't trust."

"Then it's a good time for you to practice that vow you made." He chuckled low. "See you later."

Lizzie searched her outfits. She rarely had so much trouble deciding how to dress.

Having already given him the spiel about the Red Lady, she figured her best bet would be a story he might know about. She slipped into a V-neck white pirate shirt and black pants. A blue vest that fell past her waist was next. She tied a cream-colored sash, letting the ends hang down along her thighs.

Belts and buckles followed. She donned brown slouch boots, which looked like worn leather, over her own shoes.

Assessing herself in the mirror, she whispered, "Perfect." Instead of a wig, she plaited her thick hair into two braids. The headband matched the color of the sash. Placing the brown, three-corner pirate hat on her head, she was completely in character. Except for her red hair and green eyes.

Well, no one expected her to look exactly like the pirate. The red mustache would match her braids, but the black would be truer to the pirate character. Reminding herself she was going totally pirate, she chose the black.

She arrived at the Cave at four, and obliged a couple of tourists who wanted the tour. It was good practice so she was ready and piratey when the pastor walked in, wearing black jeans and a long jacket.

His conservative haircut was a little windblown. Lizzie thought he looked so wonderful that she wished he'd take off his jacket and show his collar to remind her she could not date a pastor. She scowled. "Argh, matey. Shiver me timbers!"

He smiled, dimples denting his cheeks. Oh, no, not dimples, too! Adorable. She hadn't noticed that before. Maybe because there had been so much of him to notice … and to try and forget.

She breathed deep and gestured to the wall. "Hang your coat on the hook and follow me."

Good. She could see the collar then.

Lizzie was determined to give him a thorough tour of all the pirate hideouts and treasures. She would make a special effort to be the most intriguing pirate that Rev. Dr. Preston Bartholomew had ever met.

She led him down the hallway and slid aside the wooden bar across the door. They entered a cavelike recess dimly lit by a lantern in a wall niche. A large ship's anchor leaned at their left and a fishing net hung on the right wall, starfish caught in its mesh.

Lizzie closed the door, then waved her hand at the rounded access that gave the appearance of a cave opening. "You are entering the world of pirates of the Caribbean. I am the captain of this ship called the *Black Pearl* and we sail the seven seas."

Even in the dim light of the pirate cave, she could see the golden gleam in his dark eyes that widened. "Ah, yes," he said. "The gentlemen and ladies will always remember this as the day they almost caught Jack Sparrow."

She exhaled audibly. "You know that movie quote?"

Instead of answering, he laughed.

"What?"

Amusement sparked his eyes. "Not often I see a lip sporting a mustache."

"Oops." She felt it then. The mustache had slipped down.

How embarrassing. Here she was. In a dim cave with a gorgeous man staring at her mouth, and her lip had a fake mustache on it. At least she didn't have to worry about tempting him. She readjusted the mustache's skin-colored elastic band around her ears, gave a shrug and led him down the steps and into a tunnel.

"I do watch movies," he said.

Oh, she'd figured he wasn't allowed to do worldly things. And he liked pirates. This was getting worse and worse.

She forced herself into pirate mode. "Shall I interest you in what pirates of the past have done here?"

"Please do."

As she led him along a tunnel, she couldn't help but think about that famous line he quoted. She wondered... what if? What if he wasn't a pastor? What if she hadn't made that vow? Would he have thought her a great catch?

But what is...is. Maybe she should just go fishing...for nothing more than...fish. Her life was over. The perfect man. But, the reason he was perfect was because he was so committed to the Lord.

She always found something wrong with every guy she'd met or dated. Why did she want this man?

The answer dawned on her. Adam and Eve had had access to an entire garden, but they had wanted the forbidden fruit. That must be it.

The thought reminded her of a girl in the singles' class at church. Constantly on a diet, she always talked about the desserts she couldn't have. They were always on her mind. The forbidden.

Well, Lizzie knew there were certain lines one didn't cross.

Now that she'd lectured herself back into sanity and was getting her life into perspective, she could relate to Rev. Bartholomew as she would relate to her own pastor.

Besides, if this man were not a pastor, she'd probably find things wrong with him. Maybe she should pretend he was not a pastor.

Oh, no! If she did that, she'd surely grab him and kiss the tar out of him.

Yeah, sure—as if he'd allow that. If he ever looked at her lips, he'd remember the mustache and laugh. Her mouth would be a conversation piece, a joke, something that sported a mustache.

Lizzie led him into caves and tunnels, telling stories that were reported to be true. Caves used as morgues by hospitals. Tunnels used as hideouts during the Underground Railroad days. Caves where bodies of those who died from yellow fever in the 1800s were hidden from the general public.

He listened in rapt interest and finally asked, "Which one has the scene of the killing in DeBerry's pirate book?"

"Down this way." She led him to the cellar. "The tunnel connecting to this one leads to the Savannah River. Captains would wait for the drunken sailors, hit them over the head and drag them through the tunnel to the river. The sailor would wake up on a pirate's ship and sail off to China."

"How do you know it was China?"

She straightened her mustache, then grinned. "Because

most of the stories say the sailors were 'shanghaied.'" She lifted a shoulder. "So, where else?"

His dimples appeared, and she shuffled him off to another cave. "This is a real pirate chest." She moved aside a treasure map, lifted handfuls of gold coins, bangles, necklaces, chains and jewels, letting them clink and scatter down into the chest.

His dark eyes reflected the gold. "Imagine if that were real."

She supposed even formal pastors yearned for a life of excitement on the Seven Seas occasionally, a fantasy life they couldn't have.

He would return to his congregation and stand on a dais in a royal robe that set him apart from the everyday worshipper.

And Lizzie? She would straighten her mustache, greet her customers, and say, "Yo, ho, ho. A pirate's life for me."

They were too different to be together.

Chapter 5

Zach loved the stories, mainly because they enhanced the excitement he experienced when reading DeBerry's book. Now, this pirate lady brought it to life. No wonder DeBerry had been inspired by this place and this girl. Zach felt like a boy again, reading *Treasure Island*.

The treasure chests filled with fake gold and coins represented the gold mine he'd found. He'd found a treasure in this girl who could lead him to the one person he'd love to meet. Since DeBerry's movie deal fell through with the big company, Zach might have a chance.

And this girl was a natural...treasure? His head spun with possibilities. He could see the movie in his mind, could see the Red Lady. Yes, he had a feeling she was a treasure and his ticket to the big time. That's all it took. That one big chance. He mustn't flub this one.

"I thoroughly enjoyed the tour," he said as they ascended the steps and reached the cave recess above the tunnels. "Really cool." He laughed softly. "In more ways than one." He wasn't too sure about his acting ability, having little idea how a member of the clergy who wore collars and robes would behave. The role of pastor he had played in the film had been a small, albeit important, part. He'd needed to act dignified and reserved.

"You asked if I had any more questions," he said.

She looked up at him with those inquiring green eyes. "If I'm not asking too much, I'd like to hear more." The emotion he tried to portray was uncertainty. "Are you free for dinner?" he asked...timidly. "Would you join me? I mean, they let you eat?"

"No." Pain clouded her face making him hurt. She spoke sorrowfully. "After going into the tunnels pretending to be a pirate, a real pirate comes and I either get hanged or I'm forced to walk the plank."

He laughed as reservedly as he could. He thought there hadn't been a pirate alive who'd make this one walk a plank. Not a girl like this, so colorful to look at, adventurous and with a quick wit better than a written script.

She removed the mustache and tucked it into a pocket. Thank goodness. He'd been ready to reach out and straighten it as he had wanted to while in the tunnel. He wanted to remove it and taste those appealing lips. Lips that could smile, frown, laugh or spin a pirate's tale, or sing a silly song.

Control yourself. He needed to be astute enough to handle things in a mature manner and not make any stupid mistakes, like coming on to the friend of DeBerry's wife.

"Would you like to sit in one of the dining rooms?" she asked, opening the door leading to the restaurant area. The aroma of delicious food was a stark contrast to the cool, musty smell of the tunnels and caves.

"The front room in a booth is fine. I like the view of the river from there."

She led him into the room, gestured toward a booth,

then hung her hat on a hook. He waited for her to sit and then he sat across from her, watching her fluff her bangs over her forehead and smooth her braids down the front of her vest.

Something about her...

"Thanks, Cheryl," she said when the waitress walked up and set glasses of water in front of them. He noticed first that Cheryl wore a skull-and-crossbones-printed band around her head. As she moved to the countertop, he thought her long navy and light blue vest over a white skirt wasn't nearly as colorful as the pirate lady sitting across from him. He almost laughed at that. It wouldn't matter. Cheryl wouldn't be as colorful if she dressed exactly like this pirate lady.

Zach cleared his throat and looked at the menu. "I think I'll skip the appetizer, just get to the main meal. Suggestions?"

"Southern-fried catfish."

The aroma was already in the air, along with smells he couldn't identify, and his stomach was screaming for it. "Perfect," he said. "Haven't had that since I was here a couple years ago." He started to add that was a favorite when he was a boy, that it brought back memories of him and his grandpa catching panfish. But he needed to be careful about leading into personal questions. "Does that come with vegetables?"

"Fries and cole slaw. But you may substitute for the Cave Salad. Spring greens—"

"In the fall?"

She squinted her eyes and scolded. "It's spring year 'round in Savannah."

He lifted a reproving finger. "Except last night."

"Touché." Then she continued. "Tomatoes, cucumbers, shredded carrots and our own special dressing."

"Sounds like a meal." He closed the menu and the less-colorful pirate waitress appeared asking if they were ready to order or wanted drinks first.

"I'm ready," he said and looked across. "You first."

She handed her menu to Cheryl saying, "We'll both have the cat and the Cave salad. And…coffee?"

He nodded, handed Cheryl his menu, took a sip of water and thought the pirate lady must be waiting for the questions he'd mentioned when he asked her to join him. "Um," he said, setting his glass down. "How long have you been a pirate?"

"All my life. I remember my mom as a pirate here more than any other place. I dressed as a pirate when I was a child. I have photos of me as a baby pirate." She laughed. "But my earliest memory of it is when I was three. I'd prop up on the countertop, cross my little black-stocking-covered legs and swing my foot, which wore a pirate boot, of course. My mom would tell stories about the little girl on the pirate ship. The daughter who grew up to be a pirate. That may be why I like being a waitress and telling pirate stories."

Zach's conscience tugged at him. Maybe this was the time to say he wasn't a clergyman. They were both in costume as part of their jobs. She a waitress and he an actor and producer. But it wasn't as if they were going to connect. All he needed was an introduction to Sy DeBerry. If she discovered he wasn't a clergyman, she'd probably think it a great joke. Or she might kick him out of the place.

He already knew she had a sense of humor, spontaneity, a love of the unusual. He got the impression she'd be bored out of her skin with a so-called normal life. No, she'd manage to make normal exciting. Just looking at her was exciting. Well, in the sense that she was so vibrant. In looks and personality.

Cheryl arrived with a tray and set their coffee and salads on the table. He looked across at the pirate lady and wondered why she didn't pour cream in her coffee or pick up her fork. Oh, she'd been waiting for him to pray. There was, he hoped, a limit to how far he'd go. He gave a nod. "You do the honors?"

The honors? Why had he said it like that? He didn't think he'd ever heard anyone refer to praying that way. But she bowed her head and closed her eyes without question. Maybe she thought that's what clergymen said. Maybe it was? Who knew? Not him.

With his thoughts running amok, her words didn't penetrate except when she got to "Amen." He watched as she poured cream in her coffee, then passed the small pitcher to him. He was wondering what to ask, how to lead in to a conversation about her friends. Before he could decide, she looked over at him with those amazing green eyes. "Do you have a church, or I guess that would be a parish, near here?" She pierced a grape tomato with her fork.

As soon as she started the question, he had lifted the cup to his mouth. He should have been prepared. How far to take this pretend thing? He sipped, then slowly set the cup down, pondered it a moment. He spoke the truth. "I live in California—Malibu, in fact."

"Oh," she said, and smiled. "That accounts for your accent. It's not exactly Southern."

He smiled then. Some of his friends often detected a little of the South in him, still there from his early childhood. But he'd practiced more than one kind of accent. His Southern accent would probably sound fake now. He had to take a deep breath as the unwanted thought entered.

He focused on his salad. What did it matter? He didn't have to share his entire life history. "You might say I'm on vacation." He supposed that was true, too. He had just finished his acting job and didn't have a movie to film at the moment.

"Why are you in Savannah?" Her green eyes filled with curiosity.

He was careful to chew completely and swallow before talking. She must think him terribly polite. "Working with some colleagues on important matters," he said. "Last night, we finished late and I thought I'd stop by here for dinner."

If she drew the wrong conclusions, it was not from what he said, but what he didn't say. A matter of interpretation. He didn't have to say his colleagues were those doing the filming at the historic church when there were no services. His part was hearing the confession of a would-be killer, and the premise was whether he would divulge the confidentiality.

"And also," he said, a little more comfortable with the other truth, "I lived in Savannah until I was twelve years old. My dad has friends here that we've visited sometimes. And for the past few years I've returned for the film festival."

"You're staying with friends?"

"No. I'm at the Conley B and B, not far from here."

She seemed delighted. "I'm well aware of that house. I lived there with my friends while in college. Then Annabelle married Symon. Megan turned the house into a B and B after she married Noah." She lifted her shoulders and sighed. "Megan and Noah are in Hawaii on their honeymoon."

He found that curious. She had a friend married to a famous novelist and another who owned a B and B. But she was a waitress. Nothing wrong with being a waitress, but he didn't think college graduates usually became waitresses. Maybe she didn't graduate. Or maybe it was like Cliff said, depends on your definition of friends, real or social media. However, she obviously knew those people.

The man he'd seen last night came out wearing an apron

and a chef's hat with pirate tricorns printed on them. He set down their dinner plates. "Hope this is to your satisfaction." He seemed to hesitate as he looked at the girl and added, "Pastor."

The pirate lady exchanged a quick glance with the chef, then turned her face to the window, a faraway expression on her face. He followed her gaze and thought she was looking out over the river, contemplating.

"I'm not interfering with your work, am I?" he asked, and she turned toward him again. An amused look was on her face as if he'd said something humorous. "I mean, if that's the manager, I wouldn't want to cause you any problem."

She shook her head. "He's not the manager. And there's no problem. They couldn't do without me around here."

He laughed with her. She might be joking but he had a feeling it was the truth.

"If we have a sudden burst of customers, I'll accommodate. We aim to please."

"Mmm," he groaned. And this time he spoke before swallowing. "I'm pleased." He pointed to the catfish and to his mouth.

She laughed, apparently liking his reaction.

He casually asked about her friends, the college she mentioned, and was not surprised that she'd been a cheerleader. The friend who married DeBerry was a beauty queen, and she'd said the friend on her honeymoon owned the B and B. She filled him in on some of Savannah's history.

She had some pretty classy friends. An idea hit him like lightning from the sky. Imagine what a boon it would be for him and for this waitress if she were to be discovered by a movie producer. Meaning him.

He could almost see the headline: Producer Discovers Actress.

Finally, he took the last sip of coffee and said, "No

thanks," to Cheryl who walked close, holding a pot. He peered at the pirate lady and she looked rather as though she'd lost her best friend. Maybe he should accommodate. After last night's no-dating scene, she apparently didn't have a fiancé.

"Miss Pirate Lady," he said. "Just so you know, I respect your decision to give dating a rest. At the present, my commitment is totally to my career. So, um, since you're not dating and I'm…" He touched a finger to his collar and lifted his eyebrows, making his eyes a question. She smiled tentatively. That touch of vulnerability was attractive for a bold pirate who could swish a sword like some pro actors he'd seen. "And your friends are away."

Her eyes widened, waiting. He thought she liked him. Well, liked the clergyman.

"What I'm trying to say is the only times I've returned to Savannah have been for the film festival on Tybee Island. In your free time…" Now, how would Preston Bartholomew handle this? He took a deep breath and stared out the window, assuming a serious expression. "I'm sorry. You've been too kind already."

She laughed lightly. "You're right. I'm at loose ends right now. I'd love to accompany you to Tybee, and show you the lighthouse. I'll take tomorrow off—"

"I don't mean to take advantage." Now, there was a lie if he ever told one. But just a little white one. Just…being friendly. Nothing wrong with that. After all, he was discovering her…maybe.

He slid out of the booth and so did she.

The fellow in the chef's hat walked in from the dining room. He stopped in front of them. "Hope you enjoyed your dinner." He paused again. "Pastor."

There seemed to be some scrutiny in the man's eyes. Was he jealous? "Food was excellent," he said, taking his wallet from his back pocket.

"On the house, remember? I mentioned it last night."

"Any charge for the tour?"

"No. It's free."

"Thanks."

With people coming in, there was no time to strike up a conversation. The chef spoke. "Lizzie, a couple in the dining room would like a tour."

"Got it covered, bro."

"Thanks again," Zach called as the chef lifted his hand and walked away. The place was beginning to buzz.

He searched his bills and found no singles. Laid a five on the table. Maybe that was a decent tip for his meal. Pirate lady probably ate for free.

"Tomorrow?" he said.

She nodded. "Oh, wait. Your jacket."

She got it from the hook and held it for him to slip into. "Bro?" he said.

"Yeah. I guess we didn't do introductions last night. Too stormy. He's my brother. Paul Marshall."

Paul Marshall?

Brother?

Zach started to turn toward her. No, not a good idea just then. A memory of a little girl and her brother was taking shape in his mind, and he'd rather not deal with it.

On an unsteady breath he said, "Where can I pick you up in the morning?"

"If I'm to be your guide, let me pick you up. I'll meet you at the B and B at nine. Gotta run."

A glance over his shoulder revealed her lifted hand and smiling lips as the costumed pirate lady became Lizzie, a real girl with flame-colored hair.

She turned away before he could say more.

That was the tricky question.

What more might he say?

Chapter 6

That girl's on fire!

The words accompanied the name Paul Marshall.

The image of a little redheaded girl from twenty years ago crossed Zach's mind. Apparently the memory had clung to his mind like Spanish moss on a live oak. He hurried to his car and drove toward the B and B but it was as if a DVD had been shoved into his brain and the movie began to roll.

He was twelve years old, and he was hurting. He had hated being there, being in that church. He sat between his mom and dad, a little too old to sit between his parents. But that's where they put him, and it wasn't to feel loved, to be part of a family. He sat between them to keep them apart.

He hated the wedding. When everybody stood to watch the bride walk down the aisle, Zach thought she was too old to be a bride. But if his mom and dad got divorced and married again they'd be that old, too. His mom had whispered, *That's the senator.*

Zach thought she meant the man walking down the aisle with the bride.

His mom had already said everybody would be there. The senator would give the bride away. Zach didn't know anybody, but his mom said she was a cousin of the groom and so should be there to show her support.

The church was packed, and the reception at the big mansion was worse. Everybody was smiling. Even his parents. It wasn't that way at home. At least, not since the previous day when he'd learned about the doctor. His parents had argued. Zach felt sick now, but that wasn't the reason he kept looking around and listening for anybody called a doctor.

He knew a lot of doctors and when some introductions were being made he heard that mentioned again. His school principal was Dr. Clovis Collins. She wouldn't be the one, but he'd watched her like he watched everybody else.

People applauded when the bride and groom fed each other a bite of cake. With their fingers. This seemed strange to him since he'd been instructed to be on his best behavior.

There was a table set aside for the children, and it was filled with food. He was directed to it, but for the first time in his entire life he didn't get excited about cake and punch. He turned away from the table and saw some children going out a door, so he followed them. He walked out into the backyard, thinking about the bride and groom, wondering if they had been married before, and divorced, and were now marrying somebody else.

He remembered his mom saying, *Imagine. Brandley's business about to go bankrupt and now he's marrying one of the wealthiest women in Savannah. Talk about luck.*

His dad had said blandly, *Maybe it's love.*

She'd turned and then walked away.

Whatever it was, Zach didn't like it. Then he wondered why his mom and dad got married. He didn't know. He'd never asked. He just thought they were a family. He knew about divorce, but didn't think it was something that would happen to him.

They said they loved him just the same as if they had remained a couple. But nothing was the same. He had to choose. His mom or his dad.

How could he do that?

Zach quit pacing when he heard talking and laughing. More children were coming outside. He didn't know anybody. Didn't want to.

He was walking past the white tables with umbrellas when he heard some girls. He saw the flower girl and another girl, who took off her hat, red curls tumbling to her shoulders.

That girl's on fire was his first thought. The way the sun shone on her hair made it look like flames. It wasn't as if he'd liked her or anything. She might be five or six years old. He'd just never seen anyone so colorful.

All of a sudden two boys came out with plates and cups of punch. One stopped and stared, like Zach was doing. Then the boy singsonged, *She swallowed a quarter.*

The other one laughed and chided, *And it came out in pennies.*

They began to laugh.

She's got mud on her face.

Leave her alone, Zach warned, taking steps toward them.

One boy shoved the other, who ended up splashing the girl with punch. *Look what you did,* she screeched holding her dress.

He pushed me.

Did not.

Did, too.

It all happened in an instant. The flaming girl's next move was to thrust her hand forward and splash her punch in his face.

The boy stood, mouth wide open, as red punch ran down his face and onto his suit. Then he began to wail that his eyes hurt. His friend started to laugh. The wet boy pushed his arm. The other one pushed back and he lost his balance and brushed against the little girl. Next thing he knew she pushed the boy. He lost his balance, and she was straddled on top of him hitting him with her fists.

Stop. I can't see, the boy pleaded. He had his arms covering his face so she beat his chest.

Elizabeth!

A boy bigger than Zach ran up. He pulled Elizabeth off the boy and held her while she kicked and screamed, wanting to finish the job she'd started. The boy, with his shirt hanging out and his tie askew, rolled away and scrambled up. Both boys ran toward a big oak.

The bigger boy yelled, *You want to fight somebody, you fight me. She's just a little kid.*

Zach thought she'd done okay.

A man came out and shouted, *Paul Marshall, what are you doing?*

The boy set the girl down. *Protecting that boy she was beating.*

E-liz-a-beth... the man said in a reprimanding tone but didn't look mad.

Her fists were balled and her eyes, the color of the grass, sparked. *He got punch on my new dress.*

Zach saw her lip tremble but she breathed in deep and tightened her lips.

The man touched her back. *Let's go see Mama. She'll know what to do.* They went into the house.

Elizabeth kept looking back as she walked to the house, but the boys were hiding behind a big tree, farther back than Zach was.

We'll wash your dress, the flower girl said to Lizzie. *You'll be all right.*

Paul called to Zach, *Tell your buddies they will answer to me if they come near my sister again.*

Zach wanted to say he wasn't with them. He didn't want to hurt the little girl. He'd just watched because she was so different from any other girls he knew. She had walloped the boy. He'd never seen a girl do that.

He just nodded and looked at the ground instead of into Paul's warning eyes. Paul headed back to the house. And Zach didn't know where he should go. Not inside. Not to the trees where the boys were hiding. He scuffed the toe of his shoe on the patio and then something caught his eye. It glittered on the grass. He reached down and picked up a little silver heart with what looked like a rose etched into it.

He stared at it in his palm, then at the house. It had to be hers. He knew what it was like to try and be brave. And not cry when you felt like it. He wanted the little girl to know he wasn't with those other boys. He didn't want to hurt anybody.

Zach put the heart in his pocket, went inside and got a cup of punch. Everybody was still smiling and talking. He went back out and waited, hoping the girl would come outside again. Pretty soon both girls did, but he was disappointed. She had another cup of punch, though he supposed he could let her know he had gotten some for her anyway. Just say he wasn't the mean boys' friend.

He walked toward the girls, but before he could say anything, the flower girl said, *Go away, you meanie.*

The fire girl said, *Paul's coming.*

Here, was all Zach said and put the cup on the table. *It's for you.*

But they thought he was a meanie. So he walked away.

It wasn't until later at home when he was changing clothes that he remembered the little heart.

He didn't know who to ask about returning it. His mom and dad weren't talking. Or smiling. Since they didn't care that he was losing his parents and his home, why would they care that a little girl had lost a silver heart?

When Zach entered his suite in the B and B, the thoughts persisted. The few times he'd returned to Savannah, he remembered the exact moment when his life had been uprooted, and the wedding usually came to mind. When his mom married again, he had refused to attend. However, he didn't mind years later when his dad married Carol. He'd been older then, even if he had often felt like a twelve-year-old, deep feelings of anger and loss surfacing.

He was almost certain Lizzie was that little girl called Elizabeth. But he had to find out for sure. And he needed to pick the right time to let her know he was Zach Grant, who'd wanted to come to her rescue.

The next morning he stood on the balcony waiting for her. A sleek black sports car came into sight from around the side of the house. A waitress drove that kind of car? Maybe this was someone else, but no, there was no mistaking that red hair. He grasped the railing, looking down as she exited the car.

His breath caught, and song lyrics flooded his mind. *Elvira...my heart's on fi-uh. Elvira.*

He swallowed hard.

She was a flame standing in the morning sunlight, her beautiful face turned up toward him. She lifted a hand, smiling, and her hair rippled across her shoulders and far down her arms.

He'd never seen anyone look so...alive.

The girl was on fire!

Chapter 7

Lizzie hadn't struggled...much...with what she'd wear. She figured casual but suitable enough for a visit to the lighthouse. Ultimately, she decided just to be herself and donned jeans and a white shirt topped with a cozy light-knit green sweater.

She'd fastened gold hoops in her ears and slipped her feet into stack-heeled loafers. No need to fret. Looks weren't everything anyway, she reminded herself even as she stared up at the balcony. They were just first impressions.

But Rev. Bartholomew had a way of impressing them on her each time she saw him, and even more as he hurried down the steps from the second floor of the B and B.

With a brisk hop, he stepped onto the ground and headed across the patio toward her. Thank goodness he still wore the collar. It would stop her from thinking inappropriate thoughts.

As he came closer, she saw it wasn't a clerical collar,

but the white collar of a sport shirt showing at the neck of a black sweater. He wore jeans.

At least the black sweater would remind her he wasn't her white knight.

She remembered Paul's admonition last night when she'd told him she and Preston Bartholomew were going to Tybee. Paul had said, *You see a clergyman. I see a man with a collar.*

Unfortunately, so did she. And he wasn't even wearing one today.

"Good morning, Elizabeth," he said.

She gasped, surprised. "Why did you call me Elizabeth?"

"Isn't Lizzie short for Elizabeth?"

She nodded. She hadn't been called by her full name in years. Ages ago, most people had started leaving off the *E* when saying her name, then it had been shortened to Liz, and by the time she had become a high school cheerleader, she had been going by Lizzie. She thought it suited her better. "Nobody has called me Elizabeth since my dad died."

"I'm…sorry."

"No. I…like it." It felt like a term of endearment. And, too, his thinking of her as Elizabeth put their relationship on a more formal basis. Not that there was a relationship.

"Great car," he said, running his hand along the sleek finish.

"Not mine," she admitted. "I can take my pick of what to drive while my friends are in Paris." She huffed, as if chagrined. "And in Hawaii." She shook her head playfully, a little jealous but pleased for them. "This is Symon's."

"Yeah," he said and laughed. Then looked at her with a steady gaze. His head shook slightly. "You don't mean…?"

"What?"

"Symon…who?" His face tightened.

"Symon Sinclair."

He relaxed.

"Oh, maybe you don't know that name," she said. "His pen name is Sy DeBerry. DeBerry is his middle name."

"This?" His face tightened again. "This is Sy DeBerry's car?"

She blew out a heavy breath. "Would I lie to a pastor?"

That seemed to surprise him for a moment. Then he gave a short laugh and peered at her with dark brown eyes that reflected the glint of golden morning sun. The light breeze stirred his hair... She needed to think of something else. Stat. She lifted her chin. "Because you doubted me, I think you should pay the consequences."

His eyes questioned, so she laughed. "Your consequences are...you have to drive."

He pointed to his chest. "I? Drive Sy DeBerry's car? You're kidding me. Whoa...." He held out his hand. "Keys please."

"They're in the car." She thought he didn't really believe her but she jumped into the passenger seat, gave some general directions about the car and the route they'd take while he switched on the engine. His face assumed a satisfied expression as the car didn't even bother to purr, but rather floated toward its destination.

"Now," she said, "if you like, I'll tell you all about Symon DeBerry Sinclair."

"Like?" he said as if the word couldn't begin to describe how he felt about that. "I'd be honored."

She chuckled at his enthusiasm. Obviously, a pastor could be as much a fan of a famous author as those she'd seen at Symon's book signings. She watched Preston Bartholomew's delight as he drove while she related Symon's background growing up as the caretaker's son on Aunt B's property.

She enjoyed his rapt interest and the questions he asked as if wanting to know everything she knew about Symon.

"He became famous, returned to Savannah and stole the heart of Annabelle, our city's beauty queen."

The twenty-minute drive to Tybee seemed like two. The conversation, mainly on her part, was about Symon and his writing. They also discussed *The Pirate's Treasure*. Apparently, the pastor had absorbed that book. He spoke of being impressed by certain scenes, and he seemed as excited about the cave tour as Symon had been when she'd taken him. "*Tybee* is an Euchee Indian word for salt," she explained as the lighthouse came into view. "And in case you don't know, the word *lighthouse* means truth."

She thought he *might* know that, but maybe he didn't know her next fact. "There are 154 steps to the top." He simply nodded. "And no elevator."

His inquisitive glance met her gaze and that little groove appeared between his eyebrows. She thought he knew what was coming. "So we'll have to see who can get to the top first."

He grinned. "I suspect you can be quite a challenge."

"Everybody needs a little fun thrown in every once in a while."

He sighed. "You're calling the shots today."

When they entered, he picked up a brochure, looked at her and then the steps. "How will we get the history lessons that are presented on the way up if we race?"

She shook her head. "Nope. You're not getting out of this. We can read those on the way down."

"What about the people on the steps?"

"They move aside when they see us running. Most are good-natured about it."

"And if they're not?"

She grinned. "Their problem."

"You've done this before," he accused.

"I always bring my dates here. Good way to get to know them. Although, of course, this is not a date," she added quickly. "I'll count to three and say go. If you go too soon, you get thrown off the top."

"Deal," he said, and she liked his stance. She never liked the guys who thought they'd give her an edge or let her get a head start. She really wanted to throw them off. Instead, she never dated them again.

"Okay. One. Two. Three. Go."

She loved the way he started off like a shot, as did she. He was a step or two ahead, then she was, then they were together and laughing. There were only a few other people on the steps. Most stopped to read the history hanging on the walls. Laughing, an older man encouraged them, "Go. Go. Go."

Lizzie overtook him near the top. He was right behind her, but breathing heavily. She took deep breaths and paced a bit.

"I guess—" he had to stop and breathe "—I don't have to—" breathe, breathe "—get thrown off?"

She laughed. "So far, so good." Her heart rate was just beginning to lessen.

"I'm more out of breath than you," he admitted. "You have very long legs."

He looked at her legs? Oh, how silly. Everybody looked at everybody's everything. Even pastors knew people had legs. "Well, I'm constantly running up and down Aunt B's staircase and I use the exercise equipment in her basement." She grinned. "I don't sit in an office counseling people all day."

He shook his head. "I don't do that."

"You do look—" she began and decided she mustn't say *wonderful* so she said, "fit."

"Thank you," he said and headed for a window. "Let's see this breathtaking view the brochure talks about."

She'd already seen it, but did what she had to do and described the salt marshes, the sand dunes, the Civil War

battles and the many flags that had flown over Tybee—
the pirates, Spanish, English, French and the Confederacy.
"At the north end is Fort Screven." She told him about
the American soldiers who trained at Fort Screven during
World Wars I and II.

His face turned toward her and she expected a question, but he said, "You make history sound as exciting as
piracy."

For a moment, she couldn't tear her gaze from his. Then
he looked out at the view again. "I've had a lot of good
lessons," she said, and she told him that Megan was a historic tour director and was a great example of a history
storyteller.

"That's not the reason," he said, not turning toward
her, just staring out the window as if something were very
serious.

"Thank you," she said in case that was a compliment.

Zach smiled and glanced at the stairs. "Maybe we
should run down and see what the plaques on the wall
have to say."

"Walk," she said. The view still seemed to be rather...
breathtaking. "Getting to be lunchtime," she said as they
left the lighthouse station. "Hungry?"

"I could eat."

"I'll drive." She wanted to concentrate on something
other than blasphemous thoughts. Turning onto the road
leading to her destination, she said, "If I don't kill a man
every now and then, they forget who I am."

He backed away against the car door, his hands up in a
pleading gesture. "Are you threatening me? I'm unarmed."

She laughed, getting into her pirate mode. "Just quot-
ing Blackbeard since we're going to plunder the coast of
Tybee Island. Let me tell you about a bunch of nefarious
sea dogs that inhabit this place."

This audience of one fed her enjoyment of storytelling.

She loved watching his face so expressive as he laughed, or frowned, or squinted or shook his head. After her Blackbeard tale, she described the three-day celebration that took place on the beach a couple of weeks ago.

"Every Columbus Day Weekend," she explained, "there's a Pirate Fest here. They celebrate with music, parties, parades. Along with grog and vittles."

He laughed. "I assume that grog and vittles is something like...food?"

She nodded. "Almost there." She passed some beach houses on stilts, turned in at one and parked beneath it. "This looks like a good one for merry cutthroats and rogues to plunder."

His look was askance. "Not so sure I'm up to a visit."

She got out and shut the car door. He came around to her. "If anyone's here, he's an intruder. Well, other than Paul. But he's probably already at the Cave. He lives there." His smile indicated he knew she didn't mean that literally. She grinned back. "We grew up in this house. Paul lives here now." She led him up the steps and onto the balcony. "You may sit out here and watch the waves while I whip up lunch." She shrugged. "Or come in."

"This is fine." He touched the back of a wicker chair neatly placed opposite another at the round table. "But I'd like to come in and wash my hands." She nodded and he followed her in. "Unless you want me to help."

"Nope. I plan to impress you with my culinary abilities."

His dimples showed, making her feel like butter on a hot biscuit.

Lizzie pointed the way to the bathroom, and soon afterward heard the door open and then the front screen close.

She checked Paul's refrigerator and pantry, needing to keep her mind on the...grog and vittles.

Chapter 8

Zach returned to the porch and walked over to the white banister and held on to it even though he'd just washed his hands for lunch. An image of Pontius Pilate washing his hands flooded his mind. Did that absolve him of guilt?

Now where did that come from?

Just as quickly, the answer came. It was no secret. He grew up attending a Southern church. But the visual impression would come from movies. Gibson's *The Passion of the Christ* wasn't exactly forgettable. And it wasn't something Zach wanted to forget. He just didn't think that way often. God was God, Jesus was Jesus, and Zach was Zach.

Pretending to be a pastor likely had something to do with it, too. But he wasn't really pretending. He just hadn't told Lizzie his real name. He only needed to find the right moment. He'd thought that would have been this morning when she picked him up.

Then he'd gotten distracted by the way she looked in

the morning sunlight—as if he'd been viewing the world as a black-and-white movie, and suddenly it had switched to living color. Everything else had seemed to pale.

The pirate lady had become a little girl named Elizabeth, and Elizabeth became a reality beyond his imagination.

He'd vowed to tell her who he was. And then she said the sports car belonged to DeBerry. That jarred him into his pastor role again and his career ambitions. He could hardly believe he was driving the author's car and listening to the extraordinary stories about Lizzie's friends. No, DeBerry was no Facebook friend, and there had been no time to say, "I'm no pastor."

Most of the time he had to remind himself he was in the role of clergyman. The Zach part of him delighted in the beautiful girl who became more intriguing each time he saw her, and with each tale she told. One minute she could be serious and sweet and the next she was playing games and teasing.

Yes, she liked games. She would appreciate his... acting. Wouldn't she?

Sure. She was a terrific actor as a pirate.

When there seemed to be a chance to confess...he'd remember she wasn't dating and wouldn't be with him if she thought he was not a pastor, who happened to be visiting for a short time and would soon return to California.

A graceful seagull caught his attention. The beach house setting was beautiful. A light breeze complemented the warm air. There was a softness to the sky. A private beach. He was accustomed to playing different roles. He just wasn't sure what the script was on this one.

He'd felt like Zach Grant when they'd stood at the top of the lighthouse, a word which meant, of all things, *truth*. The truth was that Zach Grant would like to pursue this girl...if the circumstances were different. Nothing like a sweet Southern girl who claims she's not available.

But the visiting pastor couldn't pursue her.

And Zach Grant couldn't because Lizzie thought he was Rev. Dr. Preston Bartholomew.

Besides, the more he knew of her and her life, the closer he got to DeBerry, his initial purpose.

"Help," she called and he turned to see her behind the screen door holding a tray.

"Lunch, for what it's worth." She looked doubtful. The sandwiches were basically meat between slices of whole wheat bread. He suspected she wasn't confident about her culinary abilities. No matter. He was starved.

They each took their plates and what looked like vegetable juice from the tray. "Coffee later," she said, "or now, if you like."

"This is fine," he said and sat.

"If you don't like it, you can feed it to the birds." She grimaced. "Want to bless it?"

"Go ahead," he said and she ducked her head and said a simple prayer. After the "Amen," he took the paper napkin and laid it beside his plate.

He needed to do some research on praying if he was going to keep this up. Of course he wasn't going to keep this up. He could tell her the truth while they ate. Or after.

"It's roast beef," she said. "Take the lettuce and tomato off if you want. I don't claim to be a cook. Paul's the cook."

"Vegetable juice?"

She nodded, and he sipped at his juice. "Good." The first bite of the sandwich was great. Not because he was hungry but the flavor made his taste buds beg for more. He looked over and she was grinning as she ate. She knew he liked it. He took another bite and washed it down with the vegetable juice, which he wasn't accustomed to drinking, but it was good, too.

He thought this might be the time to lead in to…his real name.

"Elizabeth," he began, and she smiled. Yes, she liked being called her full name. "I appreciate your bringing me out here. Treating me as a friend. That's kind of you."

"Well, it's not entirely unselfish on my part. You see, my friends are gone. The cat and dog do their own thing. My conversations are with a grinning jack-o'-lantern."

He never knew what she might say. He liked that. Now to lead in to what he should say, but instead he took another bite, and since he shouldn't talk with his mouth full…

"This is good for me," she said. "I've given up dating. And I don't have to worry about you because you're a person in a place of responsibility, and setting moral examples, therefore you are required to be chaste."

"Chased?"

She nodded.

He looked around. "I don't see anyone chasing me." He shrugged. "Are you asking if girls chase me?"

She laughed. "Oh, no. *C-h-a-s-t-e,*" she spelled.

He wagged a finger at her. "I think the word is *celibate,* taking a vow of celibacy, you mean?"

"There's a difference?"

"Not really. Celibacy means not marrying and…of course…"

"Of course," she said.

"Chaste means never having—"

"I see," she interrupted quickly. "They basically mean the same thing."

"Basically. But," he said, "I think that only applies to priests."

She shook her head. "Sometimes I speak before I think. And sometimes I think, but it doesn't help." She lifted her hands helplessly. "My friends and I are accustomed to speaking very freely and frankly."

Her cheeks flushed red, and the freckles across her nose seemed to darken. He narrowed his eyes. "Right. It's not holy to ask if one is chaste."

"It really isn't," she agreed. "What one does before committing to the Lord is of no consequence. All is forgiven."

That got him back into his pastor mode, and he remembered the movie scene with the killer who confessed to rid himself of guilt, but pled confidentiality. "Even for a serial killer who confessed?"

She nodded. Slowly. "Even a murderer. If a person commits a crime and goes to prison and accepts the Lord, he's forgiven, but still has to serve his time."

"Then what's the point of being forgiven?"

Her eyebrows lifted. "Shouldn't you answer that question?"

He had to think on that one. Shouldn't have asked. Then he remembered something, probably from a script or movie. He used his serious face and voice. "Questions are asked for three reasons. One, to find an answer. Two, to find out how much another person knows. Three, to show how much you, yourself, know."

Her green eyes narrowed mischievously. "What was your reason?"

He held up a reprimanding finger. "Answer my question before I answer yours."

She glanced skyward and back again. "What was it?" She grinned. "You ready for coffee?"

He was glad for coffee time and didn't offer to help. He needed to think. He was making too much out of this. Maybe because of all the religious talk. And praying. Did she pray at every meal? Or did she think that's what he did as a pastor?

And that question he'd asked. He'd meant it flippantly but it lodged in his brain. What's the point of being forgiven if you still have to pay the consequences?

He hoped it didn't come up again because he didn't have an answer.

That didn't apply to him anyway. He hadn't done anything to ask forgiveness for. After all, the world's a stage and people are merely players. Man in his time plays many parts. Since those words were good enough for Shakespeare, why not Zach Grant?

He quickly dismissed the thought that Shakespeare wrote both comedies and tragedies.

The screen door opened and Lizzie came out with a small tray. His coffee had cream in it. She'd remembered. "Ah, cookies," he said. "What kind?"

She shrugged. "Don't know yet. Paul makes all kinds. Experiments. But I can assure you they are made with all natural ingredients."

"So he's a chef?"

"The best."

"And he doesn't mind our eating his food?"

"Mind?" Her face softened. "He's been my mom and dad and friend and everything. He'd give his life for me. In fact, I think he has." She looked down and picked at the cookie. She took a deep breath, then smiled at him.

He'd never seen anyone become emotional because of love for a brother. A flash of memory touched his mind. That young boy protective of his little sister all those years ago. Zach almost laughed at that. Paul had actually protected the defenseless boy from his sister. Trying to lighten the mood, he teased, "And he taught you all you know about sandwich making."

"Watch it," she warned, but her green eyes danced. Something inside him twinged, but he reminded himself he needed to watch his reactions to her.

He didn't need to be thinking those what-if's. What if he were just Zach? A single guy sitting with a beautiful girl on this porch, with a private beach in front of them?

Maybe this is the time to tell her that...he was Zach. But intuition told him she was seeing him as a pastor, a temporary friend, confiding in him, letting him see more than the surface girl, and he already knew more about her than any girl he'd ever known. He hadn't really cared to know too much about the girls he'd known.

For an instant, he felt his loss again. All these years she'd had a brother who loved her so much he'd give his life for her. He didn't doubt that. He just didn't know how it felt. Since age twelve, he'd felt bereft.

No, this was not the time to confess anything. This was not the time for a...tragedy.

He was grateful his attention was drawn to the seagulls swooping down to get their meals from the ocean. "Beautiful place you have here."

She nodded. "I love it. But after my first year of college, I had the opportunity to move in with Megan and Annabelle, before the house was turned into a B and B. I thought it was time I moved away from home and let Paul have a life of his own."

"Does he?"

"He has friends," she laughed lightly and gestured, "the ocean. The restaurant, of course. He says his life is full, and if there's anything else for him it will come at the right time and in the right place." She shook her head. "I have a knack for trying to make things happen." She let out a long breath. "But I'm working on that."

Yes, he was thinking, studying her. That's what he was doing at the moment. Waiting for the right time for honesty. Maybe this was it? He could lead in to it by saying, *Speaking of the right time*.

But she spoke again. "Most of all is his faith." Her hand moved toward Zach. "Like with you. It's the most important."

His insides groaned.

"Thinking of church," she said, but he'd rather not. "Are you visiting the area churches while you're here? You had that meeting with your colleagues."

He needed to do some fast thinking. "Well, there's such a thing as visiting pastors, you know." Quickly, he added, "And visiting pastors who take over some duties." He had gone to church a few times in his life after he and his dad moved to California. But after a while his dad's acting, then directing and then marrying took precedence.

She accepted his statements with a nod. "Are you going to your colleague's church on Sunday?"

He wrinkled his brow. "Think I should chance that killer returning?"

She laughed, as if he were kidding. But, he told himself, he was only acting. Sometimes he wasn't sure if it was himself talking or the character. Then he thought of something else. "DeBerry had a church scene in the pirate book. Is it the one you attend?"

"No. Mine's more contemporary. The one in his book is one of the historic…" and she mentioned the name. It wasn't the one where the scene had taken place.

"I thought I might visit the one with his church scene," he said, as if musing over it. He didn't want to go to hers where she'd have to introduce him.

"You're allowed…?"

He lifted his brows. "Aren't you allowed to go where you want?"

Her thoughtful look turned to pleasure. "Well…yes. God gives me the freedom to worship where I want. It doesn't depend on church rules."

"Like your brother," he said, "you're very attached to your faith."

She nodded. "I'm a work in progress."

Lizzie looked pretty finished to him, but he'd better concentrate on the cookie. And on his work. Researching

the scenes in that book, being able to discuss it on a professional level with DeBerry, give his ideas and insights.
That's what he needed to concentrate on. He needed to
stay in contact with her to get a personal introduction to
the author.

He made his voice sound uncertain. "Would you…care
to join me at that historic church?"

He could tell…before she even said it, that she'd be delighted.

Then she added. "Maybe Paul will join us. The Cave is
closed on Sunday. You two have a lot in common."

Zach reached for another cookie. What did she think he
had in common with a chef? He scoffed inwardly. Probably about as much as he had in common with a pastor.

But he was behaving. And as they headed back to Savannah, with him driving the car again, unable to keep
from glancing over at the most interesting girl he'd ever
known, he thought of just how well he was behaving.

He deserved an Oscar.

Chapter 9

"He's a lot like you," Lizzie said to Paul the next afternoon when they had a moment to speak between their duties at the Cave.

"Oh, Lizzie," he scoffed. "Are you saying he's like a brother to you?" He shook his head. "If so, you're delusional."

She stood her ground. Or rather her plank and tried to keep her voice low as she pulled him over to the wall. "He treats me respectfully. He doesn't try to impress me by talking about himself. He listens and cares what I think."

"What do you know about him?"

Duty called in the form of customers, and when they could speak a few words again, she said, "He lived in Savannah when he was a child. And he's a fan of Symon's books."

"That much is like me," Paul said. "Kitchen's calling. Let's talk more on our break."

Later, they went into his office and set their dinner on

his desk. "Much better," he said, closing the door against the sound of voices and laughter mingled with background music of yo-ho-ho's, blow the man down and songs of the sea.

"He's going to church with me tomorrow," she said with a sense of satisfaction. "You want to join us?"

"I intend to be there."

"No, we're going to the historic one that's in Symon's book. He's really a fan. He asked so many questions about the caves and tunnels. Showed more interest than anyone." She thought a moment. "Except Symon."

"Hmm," Paul mused. "Reverend Bartholomew is a little late. The book has already been written."

She stopped her fork in midair. "Are you being sarcastic?"

"I guess I am." He paused. "I don't know what you're doing, though."

She wasn't quite sure, either. "Being friendly."

"What's he doing?"

"The same," she said defensively and told him about their going to the house on Tybee.

"I knew that," he said. "Who else would leave crumbs on the counter and coffee in the pot? I do commend you for putting the cups and glasses in the dishwasher."

She wrinkled her nose at him and he just looked at her lovingly. "He has been nothing but respectful. Do you know how many guys I've had to fight off?"

He nodded. "At least five thousand, two hundred fifty-four, considering all those dating services you went through." He pointed his fork at her. "You always find something wrong with the guys. Not this one. That bothers me. Where do you think this is going?"

"Nowhere," she said quickly. "But I'm more drawn to him than any man I've ever met. I really took to Symon, but fortunately the first time I saw him he was with Annabelle and I knew they clicked, even though she didn't know that at the time, or refused to acknowledge it. I click with this guy." She stabbed her food. "But he is immune to me."

Paul's glance at the wall seemed to hit it. Then he scowled. "Lizzie, my love, you often give the impression you're scatterbrained. But we who know you, know you're one of the smartest people around. Usually."

"Brother Paul, dear," she mocked, but playfully. "I know me. I could never be the wife of a formal pastor who wears collars and robes. And if I could make him want to give up his dedication to God for me, then I couldn't respect him. He'd no longer be the same person. He'd go the way of the others. He'd be a defrocked pastor outside the realm of formal religion."

"Now you're getting sensible." He relaxed, almost.

She gave a nod of assent. "I like being with him. There's a fun side to him that I think he tries to stifle. And he makes me think." And try not to think. "He asked a question I keep pondering."

Paul continued eating and lifted his brows, waiting. Finally he asked, "What was his question?"

"He asked what's the point of being forgiven if you still have to pay the consequences."

"Doesn't he know?"

She huffed. "Of course a pastor would know. He wanted to hear my answer."

"How did you answer?"

"I didn't."

"Don't you know?"

"I thought I did until he asked. But I couldn't form a decent answer in my mind. A quick answer would be that it makes an eternal difference, but what about paying the consequences while you're still alive? How would you answer?"

He chewed for a long time. "You're right. It makes sense

you have to pay the price for your actions. But the question calls for more than a logical answer. Theology is involved." He nodded, smiling wryly. "Sounds like one Aunt B should tackle."

She nodded in agreement but still looked skeptical. "Paul, don't you like him?"

"I don't dislike him. You always want me around to give my opinion of guys you date. But this is different. I think of a pastor having a position, but is still a man learning to live his faith daily. Maybe it's the collar and robe thing." After a thoughtful moment, he said, "Lizzie, I don't know him."

She shrugged. "Well, get to know him."

He gazed at her. "I'm not the one he asked to go to Tybee with him. Or to church. Besides, why should I interrogate a pastor? You're not dating him."

All she could say to that was, "Exactly."

It wasn't until later, when she was at a table of four in the dining room that Paul walked up as she was lighting the bananas foster and said, "Be careful. You know what happens when you play with fire."

They all laughed. As if he were joking.

She thought about their conversation late that night after she returned to Aunt B's and took care of the cat and dog. SweetiePie was making her rounds of the big old mansion. Mudd was curled up on the rug beside the bed. Night breeze through the open windows cooled the room that the afternoon sun had warmed, and she pulled the covers close.

Last night had been similar. After she'd spent the day on Tybee with…him. She hadn't once said his name. She couldn't bring herself to call him pastor. And Preston might sound too familiar.

Tonight was different. She had to think about Paul's skeptical attitude, and his warnings. He'd said she was smart. She'd heard that before. And she knew she was, about a lot of things. It was a lot easier being discerning about other people. Quite another when it involved yourself. She was smart enough to know that reason didn't always win out over feelings.

Earlier, she'd kept looking for him to come to the Cave but he hadn't. She wanted to see him, spend time with him. She also knew that if you cared for a person, you wanted the best for them.

Lizzie sighed into the night. It was as if God were giving her the test of her lifetime, asking if she was committed to keeping things in perspective.

She looked up at the ceiling, then closed her eyes. God had a way of asking difficult questions.

She awoke to another beautiful fall morning. Cool, but it would warm up. Thanks to Annabelle's history as a model and style suggestions, Lizzie owned a wardrobe that pleased her. She chose a leather camel-colored pencil skirt and topped it with a short-sleeved lightweight sweater. She loved the layered colors. The sleeves were taupe and stretched from shoulder to shoulder. Across the chest and midriff were light orange stripes with a black one in the center, then a wider stripe of burnt orange that brought out the color of her hair. The taupe Ann Taylor pumps trimmed in black and sporting black four-inch heels were the perfect accessory. Along with the designer handbag. She smiled at her reflection, remembering Annabelle's advice, *Don't wear any jewelry with this. The man's eyes will go from your hair to the burnt orange. Jewelry would detract.*

That had sounded odd, but after seeing the effect, Lizzie agreed. She liked her hair, too, with the bangs being the main focus and the rest pulled back from her face and arranged high at the crown and twisted around to fall just at the nape of her neck.

There, that should do. She decided to drive Symon's sports car again. Although the pastor had offered to pick her up, she said she'd meet him again at the B and B. She didn't know what kind of car he drove but thought it was probably a rental since he came from California. He'd been impressed with Symon's.

When she arrived at the B and B, she got out of the car to remove a twig that had gotten caught in the windshield wipers. As she tossed it to the ground, she was startled to find the pastor there. Staring. "I might as well say it." He blew out a breath. "You…look…stunning."

She wasn't self-conscious very often but… "Thanks to my friend's expertise."

He shook his head. "You friend isn't wearing those clothes."

Then it hit her. He wasn't saying "she" looked stunning. The clothes Annabelle helped her pick out were stunning.

"And you," she said, "look…Protestant."

He glanced down at his lightweight beige suit, white shirt, then lifted the multicolored earth-toned tie. "This do for a historic church in Savannah?"

"Perfect," she said.

His dimples appeared. "Didn't want to clash with your hair."

She laughed. "That's what I've had to think about all my life. Imagine me in pastels?" She made a gagging sound.

His cheeks dimpled again. "Shall I drive?"

"Please do."

When they arrived at the church, the usher welcomed them and asked if they had preferred seating. "Near the back?" the pastor suggested, and she nodded. They were seated on the right, in the second to last row.

She figured he might be a tad uncomfortable in this church, and wouldn't want a lot of questions that would come his way if she introduced him. If he'd wanted that he would have worn his collar. Far down on the left she saw a few people she knew. But likely he'd want to be whisked out immediately after the service ended, or he wouldn't have asked to sit at the back.

The service was more formal than at the church she attended. But, for a pastor who wore a collar and robe it might not appear formal enough. He seemed to survey the surroundings with an interested expression, as if absorbing it. He didn't join in the singing but smiled down at her when she looked at him and smiled.

When the soloist, with soft choir background, sang "Living Water," she wondered if that touched him as it did her. Of course it would. The beautiful voice and the wonderful words reminded everyone of the need for Jesus to pour out his living water on the thirsty souls of the world. Sneaking a sideways glance she saw that his head was slightly bowed. A song like this put in perspective the world's real needs, and the responsibility of Christians.

The sermon was about the woman at the well. When the service ended, Lizzie knew she'd been right; he didn't want attention drawn to himself. She felt the light touch of his fingers at her back as he steered her gently out the door.

Come on, Lizzie. Stay in that worshipful mode.

Away from the crowd, she was glad when he moved his fingers. As they walked to the car, she glanced over at him. "Different from what you're used to, right?"

He seemed amused by the question. "You're right about that. It was…" He drew in a breath and exhaled. "Different. Very well done."

She laughed. "You make it sound like a steak."

"Maybe that's because I'm ready for lunch. Let me treat you."

"Where?"

"Your call," he said.

"Okay. But we're not dressed for it. Drive to the B and B, then I'll go change and come back for you."

"I assume this is going to be casual."

"Yep. Jeans will be fine."

Watching him drive back to the B and B she thought about Paul having said, "I don't know him."

Lizzie wanted to know him. He looked over at her and they shared a smile. Yes, she would ask him what his childhood was like, what his life was like. Why he chose to become a pastor.

Chapter 10

Casual?

The jeans were blue. The shirt was white with sleeves rolled midway up her arms. A brown-and-gold woven belt seemed carelessly looped around her waist and fell toward her hip on one side. Heels chunky and of a reasonable height.

Regardless of what she might wear, Lizzie would need a makeup artist to look anything close to casual.

Her animated face, sparkling green eyes and red hair caught up at the back of her head and falling to right above her shoulders, captivated him. Gold hoop earrings gleamed with her slightest movement.

A few minutes ago, he had felt a certain elation in knowing she'd be driving around the B and B and parking below him in the driveway. He liked standing on the balcony, looking down, seeing that first glimpse of Sy DeBerry's amazing, black sports car.

So why did he still feel that sudden elation when a less

impressive, sand-colored convertible whipped around the corner? And why the delight of watching a beautiful girl exit a car and look up at him?

He almost laughed at that. Instead, he laughed with the pleasure of seeing her, even though she'd only been gone about thirty minutes. Of course, the reason he reacted to her was because he happened to be a man who liked women, particularly one easy on the eyes. Well, not exactly easy, more like startling, but that was all right, too. A few movie stars had that effect on a person. A certain appeal.

He felt outside himself as he bounded down the steps, watching his brown-denim-covered knees take the steps, his swinging arms boasting a beige sweater. It was like being a teen again, looking forward to an excursion. As if that wasn't enough, before he could even give her a compliment, one he thought most beautiful women expected after showing up wearing a different outfit, she tilted her chin and asked with a challenge in her voice, "You ride a bike?"

Feeling a spark of playfulness, maybe because of the cool, fragrant Savannah air, he lifted his brows and grinned. "Doesn't everyone?"

That little uncertainty sparked her green eyes. "I...don't know," she drawled.

His hand went to his brow then, and he shook his head. Of course she didn't know if...Rev. Bartholomew...rode a bike. This had gone far enough. The charade would end this afternoon, and he had an idea exactly how to do it.

But first things first. "It's been a while since I rode a bike." He played the role of serious pastor. "But I've heard some things are never forgotten."

Indeed!

"We keep them here," she said. "Megan has added a few in case guests care to ride." She led him to a basement door, unlocked it and they selected bikes.

He wondered if that *we* included Sy DeBerry. But he

didn't need to overdo it. To boast that he drove DeBerry's car *and* rode DeBerry's bike might be over the top.

He chose his and after a turn in the backyard with only a few preliminary bungles, which made her laugh, decided he hadn't forgotten how to ride. They pedaled along the bricks to the historic district and parked at the City Market.

It was exhilarating, riding beside the girl with hair aflame, admiring the copper and gold highlights.

"Have you been here before?" she asked as they began their trek along the four blocks of the charming, open-air marketplace.

"Yes, with friends, to see what Savannah had to offer. But I'm not much of a window shopper. Have never eaten here."

"Well, you're in for a treat," she teased, then spoke of the restored warehouses and shop fronts that gave the impression of old and new Savannah. A guitarist and singer along one side provided entertainment. Children, chattering excitedly, brought out a not-so-pleasant nostalgia in him. When he was a small child, he'd been here with his parents but it seemed all the good memories were bittersweet.

She stopped at Café GelatOhhh!! "This," she said, closing her eyes and inhaling deeply through her adorable freckled nose, "is one of my favorite places to eat."

They were seated, and he could only stare and enjoy her exuberance—even more than he enjoyed the delicious aroma of food, which reminded him of Willamina's breakfasts. Lizzie pointed out items from the menu, reading aloud her favorites—delicious, completely organic, free-range beef, sweet iced tea.

She stabbed the menu with a finger. "And *this* line is the truth."

That word again.

"This place really does have the best lemonade in Savannah."

It wasn't his favorite drink in the world, but it was a Sunday afternoon in the South and he sat across from a Southern belle, and although he would have suspected she'd choose sweet tea, he consented to lemonade.

The description of organic, grass-fed, free-range beef hot dogs stirred his appetite, but so did the meat panini, which he ordered. She chose a vegetarian one. While they waited for their sandwiches he wondered how to lead in to…the truth, when she dazzled a smile. Her eyes changed to the color of soft grass as she asked, "What was your childhood like here in Savannah?"

His immediate thought was to say it had been a fake. The good feelings of family and fun and love had faded into anger and hurt.

The emotions came tumbling back. They'd asked him who he wanted to live with.

He had stared at them in confusion. He wanted to live with his mom and dad—that's who.

From somewhere he'd gotten the idea that men left their wives for their secretaries, so he'd asked his dad, *Are you leaving Mom for a secretary?*

His father's brow had wrinkled. *A sec—? No. Of course not.*

Zach had lifted his shoulders, anxious. Finally, his dad looked pained. *Ask your mother.*

He did. His mom talked a long time about life not always going the way you planned, and he'd understood, but at the same time it didn't tell him what he wanted to know. *But why are you and Dad breaking up?*

I just told you, she said.

No. She had talked about how some people divorce. Fall out of love. Stupid things like that.

Am I going to have a stepmom?

No. After a long time, she'd stiffly said, *It's not your dad's fault. It's mine.*

All Zach could do was go back to his dad. He stared into his father's closed-up face for a long time, until it crumpled, and he threw himself into his dad's open arms. Father and son cried together.

Are you getting married again? was all Zach could say.

No.

Is Mom?

His dad took a heavy breath. *I think so.*

It was hard. Thinking his mother wasn't a nice woman. She'd worked in the lab at the hospital. The other man was a doctor. He was settled, had a good job, a reliable income. Meanwhile, Zach's dad had said he was tired of being a gymnastics instructor and wanted to go to Hollywood and take his chances. His mom couldn't take the instability of the acting, never knowing if their financial status would be plenty or none.

Zach couldn't believe that. His dad was the greatest guy he knew. Okay, maybe his mom would choose a doctor over an actor. But not over her own kid.

He'd said to his mom, *You have to choose. Me or him.*

No, Zach, darling. Nobody can replace you. She'd drawn him down beside her on the couch and held his head against her shoulder. *You're my son, my love. Nothing can change that.*

That was an explanation. But it didn't change the heaviness in his chest, the unshed tears in his eyes, the uncontrollable trembling of his lower lip, the anger and hate that welled up in him for his mom. Her words didn't mean anything. She was giving him up, giving up his dad, giving up everything for somebody else. No words changed it.

She was abandoning him.

He'd never speak to her again.

His mom had chosen.

And so did Zach. He'd decided to live with his dad, and had never regretted it.

Zach gave Lizzie a brief synopsis of his parents' breakup, editing out the unnecessary heartbreak he had felt as a kid. "Oh, there were good times when I was really young, but at age twelve, I relegated those to fantasy, as if my parents had been merely acting like we were a happy family."

He tried not to sound morbid. He wasn't emotional. He'd gotten past that long ago. After all, he was a grown man now. Knew about life and people. And he said the word *acted* deliberately, thinking this might be the time to tell Lizzie the truth.

Zach could talk with pride about his dad the gymnast, how he had placed in the Olympics at seventeen years old. He could describe how he later became a Hollywood stuntman, and after an accident had played bit parts in movies, eventually working his way up to being a recognized director.

Zach had intended to say all that, but was distracted by Lizzie's graceful hand touching his. He noticed the large rubylike stone on her right ring finger, which he had heard meant a girl was available. In Lizzie's case, though, it might mean she was single or that she simply wore a ring on her finger.

He smiled at her touch, was about to turn his hand and grasp hers as he said, "I never really forgave my mother."

Feeling her light touch stiffen, he stared into her questioning eyes, which softened again as she smiled faintly. He thought this might be the time to say he wasn't much of a pastor. In fact, not a pastor at all. Other than on the other side of a camera. *You see,* he could say, *I get into character. Like the actor who says, Bond. James Bond. He is Bond. I can say, Father Preston Bartholomew and I am the pastor. Otherwise, I am...*

On second thought, the analogy wasn't working well for him.

So he shook his head, hoping to dispel the morbid mood. He was about to tell her not to let his tale of woe be a dark cloud on this sunny day, but their paninis arrived and they let go of each other's hands.

She must wonder what kind of pastor doesn't forgive his mother. He started as he'd remembered the question he had posed to her at Tybee Island: What's the point of forgiveness if you still suffer the consequences?

The aroma and appearance of the food caused his perspective to return. For the moment, Zach was still a pastor who hadn't learned to pray so he picked up the lemonade, took a big gulp and swallowed, then pretended a gag, pointed to her while holding his neck and closed his eyes.

After her brief blessing, he faked a cough. "Now I know the meaning of too much of a good thing." He smiled at the glass. "It's truly the best lemonade I've had in years."

She snickered, and her nose twitched slightly. "Have you had lemonade recently?"

He shook his head. "I cannot tell a lie."

No, but I can live one. He banished that thought with an all-is-well expression. "Appreciating lemonade is much like learning to ride a bike again." Then he bit into the panini and could truthfully mumble its accolades.

As they ate, he focused on the activity around him, the sound of voices, the smell of good food, the music outside the café and the lemonade that really was wonderful.

"Are your parents still alive?" she asked.

He chewed thoughtfully. He'd never talked about his mom to anyone except in a few short remarks. All he'd intended was to lead in to his confession. But he was on his best behavior and couldn't very well say he didn't want to talk about it. "Yes, my dad's in California, and my mother's here in Savannah. She married Dr. Martin Scroff. They work together. He's in private practice now. Don't know if you know of him."

She shook her head. "No. But I'll pray about each of you."

He bit into a chip, hoping he didn't bite his tongue. Didn't she know it was about twenty years too late? This probably wasn't the time to ask what would be in her prayer.

He'd remembered eighteen years ago when he had found out that his mom would marry Dr. Scroff. How could anybody marry a Scroff when they could be a Grant? He really didn't know. He hadn't cared about making that lifetime commitment his parents had made and thrown aside.

His discomfort was dispelled as Lizzie began to talk about gelato. "It's Italian style. Gelato comes from the word *gelare,* which means 'frozen.'"

"Wow," he said, which made her laugh. The color in her cheeks deepened, but she went right on reading from the menu about no eggs, minimal cream—meaning low-fat—no tongue-coating, explodes in your mouth.

"Wow," he said again.

Her glance was reprimanding, but he saw the upward turn of her lovely lips. What was that? Apple red? Georgia-clay red? He hoped she couldn't read his thoughts. She continued with the menu. "Straciatella, gianduja chocolate, dulce de leche, panna cotta, ricotta cheese, fig and hazelnut." She looked him in the eyes. "What will it be?"

He certainly didn't want the ones he understood. "The first, of course," he said as if he knew what it was. "And the Italian gourmet coffee."

She ordered the straciatella without hesitation and added, "Cream with those coffees please."

To him, it seemed as if the two of them were just sitting there smiling at each other for some strange reason. Then Lizzie's eyes shifted to the side and slowly back. "I had a really rough time after my parents were killed in a boating accident. It was a shock. You just don't expect that." She paused for a moment. "But I had to accept it. I wonder if it might not be harder when they separate from you but are still living."

He'd never thought about that. She smiled wanly and continued, "I've heard divorced people say things like that. And Aunt B talks about the son she gave up when she was sixteen and how hard it was to know he was in Paris, but she wasn't allowed to know anything else about him. Oh! She talks about it freely, so I'm not telling anything she wouldn't."

He nodded and welcomed the intrusion of gelato and coffee. He'd welcome being spirited off to Italy about now. He wasn't accustomed to deeply personal conversations like this. Maybe the frozen gelato would cool it.

But after a bite and a sip of coffee, he thought he could learn to pray about things like this. "Wow," he exclaimed, and she threw her head back, laughing delightedly.

"You speak easily about your loss," he said, surprised he thought to say that.

She smiled. "I accept it. I'll always miss them, but I think of the good times. And I have wonderful supportive friends. Aunt B has a way of putting things in perspective. And of course, as you would know, there's God's love and His presence."

What could he say but, "So true."

It seemed the harder he tried to get out of this, the deeper he got into it. Zach could see she was a serious, deep thinker, had a wonderful outlook on life, was outgoing and fun. With the gelato smooth, flavorful and light on his tongue, maybe it was time for a lighter discussion.

Just then, his phone rang. Seeing that it was his theatrical agent, he excused himself from the table and walked over to a quieter corner. Fredrickson said he'd arrived at the hotel, met up with a few people and Zach's name was coming up in conversations. "The buzz is that you're one of three being considered for the lead in *Loving Life*," his agent said. That surprised Zach. The other two candidates were already known as leading men. The lead would be opposite the female who was a sure thing for a box-office hit.

"I'll be there for dinner tonight."

He returned to the table. "Sorry. That was a friend who's arrived for the film festival."

"Oh, do we need to leave?"

"And waste something like this?" He picked up his spoon. The gelato was melting but still tasty. He didn't want to leave it. He was enjoying talking and relating to her without wondering where it might lead. Certainly not where most of his relationships led when he got along with a young woman this well.

After finishing the gelato, he looked at her. "I have plenty of time before meeting him at the hotel for dinner."

"Oh. So you'll leave the B and B?" Her eyes registered what seemed to be concern. Or disappointment? Just as quickly her expression changed. Now she looked at him resignedly as a woman of moral stature would look upon a friend, who was a pastor, and…maybe didn't want him to leave?

Zach focused on his empty dish, the empty cup. The thought of leaving her made him feel as though he were watching a great movie and couldn't stay for the ending.

He'd like for her to be with him. To let her see what he did, to get excited about it. But first he'd have to tell her his real name. That could mess up everything. He'd let this charade go on too long.

But he was between two great opportunities. If he hadn't stumbled onto the fact DeBerry's movie option had fallen through, he'd be overjoyed about the possibility of the lead in *Loving Life*.

He knew he wasn't a great actor. He liked acting occasionally and it was extra money. He thought of a well-known actress who had turned to producing. When interviewed, she said she didn't want to ride the ship, she wanted to steer it.

He understood. An actor could be widely acclaimed one day and forgotten the next. A producer kept on steering the movies to the public. That is, after they became accepted in the right circles.

Producing DeBerry's pirate book into film could do it.

His mind was muddled. He'd thought he was a clear thinker. Now he was filled with confusion. He felt different. He *was* different. And if it weren't so serious, he'd laugh about the situation. Maybe it was because he had stepped into his character too much. Was behaving the way he thought a man of faith and morals might, seeing a woman as something other than either a part of a production or for personal pleasure.

"Ready to go?" he heard Lizzie say. He didn't know if he'd answered her question about the B and B. He didn't even know the answer. Everything seemed to be...up in the air.

He gazed at her a moment longer, wondering if this was the time to clear things up. Just as quickly, he'd realized it wasn't. A coherent thought developed, and he stood. No, if he told her he was Zach Grant, and she thought it was humorous and clever and fun...which brought doubts... then she'd accompany him to the film festival.

What would happen?

Any producer seeing her at the festival with him, would likely try and steal her away. Particularly if they knew she acted as a pirate or knew DeBerry. Especially after watching how she lit up the world, made things as bright as the Christmas decorations people were putting up all around town.

No, he needed to keep her hidden if possible. They'd work things out later. When she discovered he was a producer and she had potential as an actress, all would be well.

Chapter 11

The late afternoon sun played peekaboo in and out of the gathering clouds. Lizzie shivered at the chill in the air as they pedaled back to the B and B.

As they parked the bikes side by side in the racks in the basement, she inhaled deeply, trying to rediscover the pleasant scent of Preston's cologne, or maybe aftershave, she'd noticed earlier. She now detected only the scent of warm skin, perhaps her own.

Her thoughts were as divided as the basement looked: deep shadows on one side and a rectangle of sunlight spilling in through the open door on the other.

Was he as eager to meet with his friends as she was at the thought of reuniting with her friends when they returned from Paris and Hawaii? Sure he was. She'd watched him at Café GelatOhhh!! when he'd walked away with his phone. He had an expressive face, the kind of face *she* had, according to her friends. One that showed inner feelings. When Preston was on the phone, his face expressed surprise, then delight. Upon returning to the table, however, he appeared indecisive. Probably on how to kindly let her know he should withdraw from this interlude and get busy with his friends and…his business.

This was likely goodbye. She wished she could accompany him to the film festival, watch the golden flecks in his brown eyes as he laughed, hear his mesmerizing voice, a voice she sensed would have a comforting effect on someone seeking his counsel. She was glad to think of a pastor having fun. Of course, he was a person like everyone else.

She felt rather stiff as they walked outside, silent. When they reached her convertible, she turned toward him and leaned against the car.

Mirroring her feelings, the sun hid its face behind several clustered clouds, as if refusing to shed light on how to say farewell with her lips—no, not lips but voice—while her heart wished he could stay.

Lizzie wanted to be in his life, but knew it had to be as a friend only, which seemed such a trite description, considering the depth of feelings she had for the man. Of course there was the physical appeal of an extraordinarily handsome man, accompanied by her great respect for his chosen profession.

Frankly, she was surprised that she felt this way about him. Maybe it was his being so different from the men she was accustomed to, although her first requirement had always been that they be Christian.

Maybe she was influenced by that first impression she'd had of him, being swept in by a hurricane, looking like a swashbuckling pirate dressed in black, coming to fulfill all her fanciful, action-filled dreams.

He was the exact opposite from that first impression.

"Thank you for today," he said. Although the sun wasn't shining, she felt warmth on her face—it was because of the dimples in his cheeks, the tenderness in his brown eyes.

He emitted a soft laugh, then spoke as if surprised. "In fact, the last five days have been…unexpected. Different. Really quite wonderful."

Yes, she supposed he wasn't accustomed to spending several days with a woman unless business or church related.

Her eyes seemed locked with his. Five days. Somehow it seemed like a lifetime, and she didn't want it to end. This was different for her, because she didn't spend that much time with a man. She knew right away when one wasn't for her. This one, she knew, wasn't for her, but because of a different reason. And yet…she would love to repeat those five days over and over. Be his pirate. Visit the lighthouse. Sit on the balcony of the beach house and gaze out over the ocean. Watch the seagulls. Walk along the beach. Ride around in a car. Go to church together. Talk about their faith. Ride a bike through the historic district. Enjoy the City Market.

Reality seeped in. "You'll return to California soon?"

"I don't know exactly when," he said. "A lot depends on what happens with my friends at the festival. And I need to call on some of Dad's friends."

"And your mom," she added, thinking that went without saying.

However, his face clouded, maybe a reflection of the darkening sky. A drop of rain hit her cheek. "No," he said, "I don't see her often."

"Oh." Staring down at the bricks between their feet, she could imagine how stressful it must be to know your mother is right there in the same town and you can't relate to her. Probably worse than accepting the finality of death. Lizzie had the assurance she'd be with her own mother in eternity. How painful for him if he didn't feel the same way. Her eyes met his again. "Does your mom have a strong faith?"

He shifted from one foot to the other and his face closed off, brown eyes darkening.

"If that's too personal—"

"No," he said quickly. "I'm not sure how to answer." His gaze moved beyond her. "She goes to church."

How difficult it must be to wonder about one's own mother. She expected his mom would be very devout.

Lizzie didn't think she was spiritually or theologically mature enough to continue this conversation so she asked, "So, is this goodbye?"

"I won't leave without seeing you again." Both hands encircled her arms as if rather desperate, and she thought he was moving closer. The breeze stirred his hair, giving him an even more appealing windblown look.

She lifted her face, lost in the deepening brown of his eyes, watching the way his lips parted slightly as he drew in a breath. She saw the troubled brow, and as their bodies touched ever so lightly, his lips grazed her bangs, the tip of her nose.

She closed her eyes, waiting.

Oh, she didn't want to beg. Well, she *did* want to, but hoped she wouldn't. A picture flashed in her mind: Meggie in *The Thorn Birds,* groveling on the ground, holding on to the robe of the priest, begging him to love her. She didn't know if that was from the book, the movie or her imagination. Regardless, it needed to disappear.

Before his lips reached her waiting ones, she moved away. He emitted a sound, perhaps a rebuke to himself, and stepped back, dropping his hands to his sides.

She stood looking at him. "It's raining. And the convertible's top is down."

"I'll help you put it up."

Soon she was in the driver's seat, her hand on the door with the window down. He gently grasped her hand in his.

His voice low and deep, he said, "I will see you after the festival. I'll explain."

He squinted as the rain fell harder and he moved away. She turned the key in the engine and the car hummed. He ran to the steps beneath the roof and lifted his hand.

Lizzie waved and drove around the house, passing by the B and B where she no longer lived, away from the man with whom she would no longer relate.

She turned on the windshield wipers, and remembered that in each life a little rain must fall. At least, that's what the poet wrote. It happened, even when you were in a convertible with the top securely fastened above you.

Then she remembered he'd said he would see her again—and explain.

What would he explain?

The reason his lips almost touched hers?

Did that require an explanation?

Had that been only her weakness of the moment?

If it had been his, too, it was because he was human. And such a grand one. He had human feelings. A person is not a title. Pastor is his calling. She had a calling, too, to be a fine Christian woman, and she often failed miserably.

It wouldn't be easy changing her mind-set from having romantic notions and trying to find Mr. Perfect, to letting go of that dream. Some things took a little time. She had a feeling this wasn't going to be instant.

She had made a vow to God. He sent a man she would like to be Mr. Perfect—if he had been that swashbuckler the hurricane had swept in.

But he wasn't.

She'd passed the test of not begging him to abandon his calling and love her.

Now she knew she was fated to be a spinster pirate forever.

She felt as if she'd buried her treasure.

And would now sail off into the sunset…alone.

* * *

The rain had stopped by the time Zach had changed into clothes more suited for a film festival. He loved the excitement of an event such as this, people of like minds who understood how one another thought. They weren't considered strange because everything and everyone could be a plot or character in a film.

When he was younger, he'd thought himself different, but then he'd learned that making stories from life experiences was a welcomed kind of difference.

During dinner with his agent at the hotel, Zach thought about telling Lizzie the truth. Maybe he didn't need to explain, just tell her he'd gotten caught up in the role he was playing and had taken it too far. After all, she understood about getting into character. She did that with her pirate portrayals.

Silently, he explained it to himself, but uneasiness crawled around his midsection. Maybe it was the food.

He was half listening to the agent, whose eyes roamed the room for anyone representing an opportunity. That was his job. "I thought you'd be more excited about this," Fredrickson said after a few moments of silence ensued.

"The role in *Loving Life?*"

Fredrickson's expression seemed to say, *Duh.*

Zach laughed it off. "Nothing in this business is a sure thing. You know I'm aware of that. Besides—" he shrugged "—Darren and Mario are a lot better known than I am."

"Yes, but you might try looking more like a leading man than somebody who's lost their best friend."

Lost his—? Just a cliché. Zach laughed at that and put on his happy face. "I'm listening. Give me the details."

Zach had to admit, it was a great opportunity. But it didn't excite him as much as the prospect of producing *The Pirate's Treasure.*

"You know if my documentary wins the award, I'll have more chance at producing."

"Yes, but keep all doors open. You've been acting and producing."

Yes, producing documentaries, small films, all good on his résumé, but not the big one yet. His documentary, which was a finalist at the film festival, had garnered him enough attention so that he'd been asked to be on panels, as well as present a couple of workshops on acting and producing. Plus, being a presenter at the festival brought him more attention, possibly boosting his career.

"There's Spillman, who can sign you up for the lead," Frederickson said, interrupting Zach's thoughts. "Look good."

Zach laughed to himself. The routine was to stay up late, talk to everybody who was anybody, be too pent up to sleep, rise early and be ready to charm and impress the forty thousand people who invaded Savannah for the festival.

It entered his mind he would have liked for Lizzie to be among that number. He felt sure she would love the festival; she'd like to be part of this world and the excitement of turning dull and boring life into fiction, fantasy and happy endings.

If he'd told her who he was, they could have a great time here. He could share it. Let her know his hopes and dreams and lifestyle. He'd like to have someone special to share it with. He'd always shared it with his agent, and friends, sometimes with a woman who was looking for her own chance at fame.

But he needed to get his mind back to where it belonged. His intention was not to have a relationship with a woman, unless temporary. Not that he was thinking of more. It's just that he hadn't expected Lizzie to invade his mind. It had been Rev. Dr. Preston Bartholomew who'd appreciated her beauty, personality, faith. It was a boy's memory of a girl teased by meanies who spilled red punch on her frilly dress. He'd wanted to show he was different. He didn't want to see her hurt because he'd known what that felt like.

He shook away the thoughts. She was not five and he was not twelve. She was a grown-up and he was a mature man.

Really?

What was mature about letting a misconception go too far because it seemed to be to his advantage? Then again, what harm was there in it?

He's a producer, auditioning her for a great part in a movie. She'd love that. She'd be...delighted.

All the girls he knew would be. And Lizzie had natural ability; it didn't come from some acting school. She'd been performing like a pirate since...what had she said? Since she was just a toddler. Yes, he'd not only stumbled on the fact DeBerry's story was available for him to pursue, but he'd discovered an actress. That's what people in his business did. Nothing underhanded about it. Everyone involved would gain.

Well, maybe he was keeping his identity secret a little too long. But, if she liked him, she'd be glad he wasn't a formal pastor committed only to his church.

She obviously liked the pastor or she wouldn't have spent time with him. But it really wasn't the pastor, it was Zach. So she was really spending time with Zach. It was Zach she liked.

But...Zach wouldn't have weighed his actions and words as carefully. He was more free-spirited. She'd probably like Zach even better than Preston Bartholomew. Shoot, he was Zach.

He'd almost messed up when they stood in the rain and he held on to her arms. He'd wanted to kiss her. He thought she wanted that, too, and he wasn't sure who stepped away first.

She hadn't seemed to hold that against him.

So, with that private lecture, he got into the swing of things. Enjoy the present and look forward to the possibility of DeBerry's movie, Lizzie as an actress and, if that didn't work out, getting the leading role in *Loving Life.*

The film festival was phenomenal. Whenever Spillman was near, Zach raised an eyebrow, made his eyes look dreamy, lifted one side of his mouth to form a crooked smile in a way that was supposed to appeal. Sure, he could. He'd practiced enough.

But what he was most interested in was the night of the awards. There was more than a hundred thousand dollars in cash and prizes, and he wanted to win the Film Producer Award for Documentary.

When the introduction of the film was announced, Zach thought it probably came across as too dull and boring. It was about earthquakes in California, as a result of the state being located on the San Andreas Fault. Much of the film's focus was on two earthquakes: the largest —the 1857 Fort Tejon, with a magnitude of 8.0, and the 1906 San Francisco earthquake, which had been the most destructive with a 7.9 magnitude, resulting in more than three thousand deaths.

He knew it looked good, and he had included great information. But unless the earth had begun to shake when the judges made their selection it might not make a difference. Just then the building *did* begin to shake. Or was that him?

Whatever. When his name was called as the winner, he looked at Fredrickson who nodded and stood to shake his hand, while others did the same, including Spillman. He had won! He really had heard his name. He walked to the front and accepted the award.

Zach was no longer stuck between student filmmakers

and award-winning professionals; he was one of the recognized pros. Didn't matter now if his smile was crooked or not. His dimples would be showing of their own accord.

Later, as he left the celebration, he heard someone call his name. He stiffened. He knew she'd be there. She'd sent a congratulatory note upon learning he was a finalist. Turning toward her he said, "Hi, Mom," and nodded at Dr. Scroff.

His mom said the usual: she was proud of him, congratulations, and such. He could respond almost as cordially as he did to others who were happy for him. After all, he was an actor.

The ensuing days were filled with the excitement of filmmaking, which was a world unto itself. He stayed at the hotel a couple nights instead of returning late to the B and B. As the week wound down, he needed to think about seeing some of his dad's friends, then get to the business with Lizzie.

On the last day however, he could hardly believe what was happening. As he walked through the hotel lobby, three men looked his way and one appeared to indicate Zach. A man left the group and headed toward him. Zach recognized his face from TV interviews, on the internet and gracing the back of the book lying on his bedside table at the B and B.

"Zachary Grant?" the man asked, extending his hand. "I've been wanting to meet you. Sy DeBerry here."

Chapter 12

Lizzie wasn't one to have pity parties, and she sure didn't want to start looking like Smiling Jack whose huge mouth had begun to droop. She would love the excitement of the film festival. The idea occurred that she might call a friend from church and they could attend together.

But on second thought, it wasn't a film or the crowds that brought on that urge. It was the pastor. She couldn't show up there as if she was stalking him, which, to be honest, was exactly what she'd be doing. So she lectured herself, not as well as Aunt B might, but knowing the facts of life and what can and cannot be, she threw herself into her job at the Cave.

The Cave was always packed during the festival and movie people loved touring the tunnels and caves. Some even said she ought to be in movies. She liked the compliments. She didn't have time to give much thought to Preston Bartholomew.

Except late at night after she'd climb into bed and say

her prayers, which included him. She looked forward to seeing him for a final goodbye. Maybe they could correspond occasionally.

Her phone seemed exceptionally silent and she received no text messages. But then, it wasn't as if they should communicate. He'd said he would spend time with friends at the festival and visit relatives.

Her thoughts moved to her own friends after Annabelle called to say they would see her in a couple of days.

On Friday night as she maneuvered the car onto Aunt B's property and up the long drive beneath the moss-laden oaks, she delighted in seeing the lights shining from the cottage windows and blazing from the mansion. She smiled at the sight of Mudd and SweetiePie cavorting around the front yard, reacting to their owners' return.

Lizzie wanted to cavort herself. She loved seeing the porch light on, knowing someone was inside waiting for her.

The aroma of hot chocolate met her as she opened the kitchen door, but more delightful was the open arms of Aunt B, ready to envelop her with love.

They sat at the kitchen table, sipping their chocolate, Aunt B looking beautiful but tired, saying there was so much to tell. Symon had just returned from taking Henri to the B and B.

"I didn't know Henri was coming back so soon," Lizzie said.

"I couldn't be certain," Aunt B said coyly. Then she thrust forth her hand. On her ring finger was a beautiful sparkling diamond reflecting the light in Aunt B's eyes.

"Oh, it's gorgeous," Lizzie said. "But not unexpected, is it?"

"Not entirely," she said. "But Henri and I needed that time in Paris to see how we would relate at his villa and in the places where our son grew up." She closed her eyes and shook her head. "I won't share everything yet. The others will want to be in on the conversations. I'm truly exhausted, so let's get our rest and talk all day tomorrow."

Lizzie loved that idea, although she would have liked to hear everything right then, and tell Aunt B about her new commitment to the Lord.

Sleep did not come readily. Mudd would be snoozing at the bedside of Symon and Annabelle. SweetiePie came in, but went out again and would likely end up with Aunt B. When would Aunt B and Henri marry? Would Lizzie need to move back in with Paul? Oh, so many things unsettled.

Only about her life. The others were settled. Megan and Noah would return from their Hawaiian honeymoon on Sunday.

Early Saturday morning Lizzie was up and ready when Annabelle called and said, "Don't eat without me," and soon came running across the back patio, appearing in the kitchen breathless and beautiful. After screaming and hugging, they settled for coffee and quiche that Aunt B had made.

"Symon coming up?" Lizzie asked.

"No," Annabelle said. "He wants to see a few people at the Film Festival. This is the last day. Then he'll need to bring Henri to get Aunt B's car, and we'll work out transportation from there. Symon and I can manage with one vehicle."

"Megan's or Noah's are available, too," Aunt B said, which reminded Lizzie of the wonderful way they all shared whatever they had, including houses or cars.

Aunt B's eyebrows lifted as she said in an exaggerated tone, "At Henri's villa in Paris, it's a matter of which car will be driven by the chauffeur." She quickly added, "But you know that doesn't impress me. What does, is the orphanage Henri supports. And he volunteers at a clinic where parents can't afford to pay for their children's surgeries." She heaved a deep breath. "That's the kind of man one falls in love with." She paused. "What's wrong, Lizzie?"

"Nothing. Why?"

Aunt B gave her a look. "I know you, sweetie."

"Right," she admitted. "I haven't been able to find the man I should fall in love with. And then, the wrong man comes and I could—if allowed—could fall in love. But it's not love. It's great respect. He's so…so…perfect."

"Then what's the problem?"

"He's a collared, robed, formal pastor who lives in California."

"Oooohhh," they both howled or meowed or something akin to the animal kingdom.

Annabelle said, "Lizzie. You need to see a therapist. There's something in you that won't let you fall in love."

"No, no. I can. I mean I could. But Mr. Perfect is Mr. Wrong because he would require a wife to live the kind of lifestyle I'm not cut out for."

"Something in you is blocking your emotions," Annabelle said. "You have a fear. Maybe of being abandoned because your parents died."

"Oh, Annabelle. Your parents died. And you aren't blocked from loving Symon. Megan's mom and grandmother died, but she fell in love with Noah even after she was abandoned by Michael and still grieving over the loss of her grandmother. I'm no more blocked than you two."

Annabelle looked askance. "There have been some nice fellows from the Christian Singles Service."

"Nice fellows?" She almost screamed. "You want me to marry somebody because they're nice?" Of course they didn't, but before they could answer, she spoke adamantly. "I have this all worked out. I'll share it when we get together and talk about what's been going on in our lives."

There was time for the bare minimum of sharing, but

of course they'd have their great dinners and share everything. In the meantime, it was Saturday, and Lizzie was needed at the restaurant all afternoon and evening.

She kept thinking Preston Bartholomew might come in, but also kept reminding herself that he had other things to do. On Sunday morning they all went to church, and Annabelle and Symon had lunch somewhere in town with his agent who had attended the festival.

Aunt B said she and Lizzie could whip up a light lunch for themselves and Henri, then sit on the front porch in the rocking chairs with their sweet tea and Lizzie could help them decide where to go on their honeymoon.

After lunch Aunt B said, "Paris is a wonderful place to honeymoon."

"Ma chérie," Henri said in that deep, musical, romantic language. "That is our home now." He paused. "Other than right here. Our honeymoon must be a place we've never been before." He leaned forward to look past Aunt B. "What do you think, my Lizzie?"

Lizzie had been thinking that Annabelle and Symon were such a happily married couple, so right for each other. Megan and Noah would return from Hawaii tomorrow. Aunt B and Henri, in their sixties, were in love, and she…?

She reminded herself that she would not despair of feeling left out. She could live wherever she liked. Stay at Aunt B's even after they married. Spend time at their villa. Move into the B and B. Live with Paul. Get her own place…anywhere.

Yes, that was positive.

"I really haven't been anywhere." She shrugged. "Except in my dreams."

"All right," Henri said. "Where in your dreams would you go?"

"A convent—" she began and Aunt B interrupted.

"Lizzie. Are you getting depressed over all this marriage and honeymoon talk?" She took a deep breath and said to Henri, "I'm sure you know by now she's been in a dither to find her Mr. Perfect and it just hasn't happened."

"That's changed," Lizzie said. "I'll tell you about that when we get together to hear about all of your experiences. After Megan and Noah return."

"What's changed?"

"I'm not looking for Mr. Perfect anymore."

Aunt B didn't comment, but Lizzie watched her head turn toward Henri and her shoulders lifted. Lizzie could imagine their gazes rising to the porch ceiling.

"Okay, what about Tuscany?" Lizzie said, then laughed. "That just popped into my head. I know nothing about Tuscany. But I like the sound of it."

Henri set his iced tea down and picked up his laptop. "I've been to Florence, but not Tuscany." He read and gave an account of the city.

"Sounds wonderful," Lizzie said.

"Yes," Aunt B agreed. "But the description reminds me of Paris and your villa, Henri."

He nodded. "Yes, there are similarities and differences. And Tuscany is only five to six hundred miles from Paris. We could hop over there anytime. My idea may not be the place for a honeymoon but at some time we might go to…Israel."

"Perfect," Aunt B said, looking out across her beautifully manicured lawn at the Spanish moss swaying on the live oaks, as if dancing with a great idea. Her face and voice were soft. "This property in Savannah and your villa in Paris are honeymoon settings. Since our lives will be a perpetual honeymoon, why not take a more serious trip to the Holy Land?"

Henri's hand reached over, and he held hers on the arm of her rocking chair. *Yes,* Lizzie thought. *The Holy*

*Land would be a particularly perfect trip for...anyone...
committed to the Lord.*

The following day, Megan and Noah returned to their
house. They, too, were anxiously awaiting the reunion dinner when everyone would be together again to talk about
their experiences. Even Paul was taking the night off from
work to join them. Symon said he'd like to bring Zachary
Grant, a producer he had researched and met at the Film
Festival, if that was all right.

Of course it was, and then he made a comment that he
liked the fellow, wanted their opinion of him, and he just
might be the type to interest Lizzie.

"Let's look him up on the internet," Annabelle suggested while Megan's head bobbed in assent.

Lizzie lifted her hands. "Nope. Maybe this is the time
to tell you about my commitment." She told them about her
vow to give up looking for a husband. At first they looked
doubtful, but eventually they were convinced.

Aunt B said, "That's very courageous of you, Lizzie. I
know you've joked around about Mr. Perfect, but it's been
serious, too. And with all of us falling in love and getting
married, it must have been difficult for you."

"Oh, I'm pleased—"

"We know that." Aunt B waved away any explanation.
"But still, we each have our own heart's desires. Look how
long I've waited...well, I didn't exactly wait. But look how
long before the real love of my life was *in* my life." She and
Henri exchanged affectionate looks. "We can despair in
not knowing. But when we can look back, we see the Lord
really did know best. But I know it's hard going through."

Lizzie sighed. "I want what's best for me and it might
not be a man." She grimaced because that idea was as sour
as if she had bitten into a lemon.

They laughed, but she knew they thought she'd made
the right decision. She would not be thinking of finding

Mr. Perfect. No matter what this film producer looked like, he couldn't look as appealing as her swashbuckler in black. Nor could he have the faith of a pastor committed only to his church.

Symon said actors and producers dressed much like he did most of the time, casual, even wore bright colors and suspenders on occasion.

"Well, then," Aunt B said. "This sounds like a Willamina's Southern comfort kind of dinner."

With that settled, the date was set. A couple nights later, Willamina began putting items on the sidebar in the dining room. As usual, she made a point of making sure her "girls," as she called them, met her approval. Aunt B wore black pants and an amethyst silk blouse that showed off her beautiful eye color. Annabelle, who couldn't look anything but gorgeous, wore a navy cowl-neck blouse over navy stretch-cotton pants. The simplicity was beautifully accented by a red leather belt and small diamond earrings. Her dark hair was pulled back in a sophisticated twist.

Megan was her classically beautiful self in indigo denims topped with a white cotton blouse. She proudly displayed the gold plumeria earrings, centered with a diamond, which her new husband bought for her in Hawaii.

Lizzie didn't consider dressing to please a man, but to please herself. She chose comfortable pants and topped them with a V-neck, shawl-collared blouse in a firework print. She simply brushed her hair, the locks falling long and loose below her shoulders.

"You girls are looking good," Willamina said.

"Thank you," Aunt B said and grinned before the rest of them had the chance. Willamina rolled her eyes and went about her business.

"Oh, I believe I hear Symon and his guest coming in," Aunt B said. Paul, Noah and Henri were out back on the patio.

The women turned to leave the kitchen and headed for the living room when Willamina said, "Miss Lizzie, something I want to say to you."

Lizzie knew if something were amiss about her, Willamina would let her know.

Willamina's brow was troubled. "Everybody's been too busy to talk much but I've been hearing bits and pieces. And I'm wondering what you're doing running around with that Hollywood fellow."

That sounded like an accusation, but Lizzie had no idea what she meant. "I don't—I'm not— What are you talking about?"

"You picked him up in Symon's car. I watched you from the window. With Megan and Noah being gone I had to know what's going on with those people at the B and B. We don't allow just anybody."

Lizzie knew that. And she would expect some film festival people would stay there. But not— She shook her head. "He's not Hollywood."

Willamina's stolid expression said differently. But maybe as she grew older, her hearing wasn't too good.

"Do you know his name?"

"That's my job, honey. Zachary Grant."

Lizzie emitted an uncomfortable laugh. "That's the name of the producer Symon's bringing tonight."

Willamina's eyes bore into hers. "Two of them, huh?"

Lizzie was shaking her head. She was feeling stupid. Didn't really want to ask the questions. Didn't want to know. She had to ask. "Do you have a…" she squeaked. "A…formally dressed pastor…staying at the B and B?"

Willamina sighed. "Not a real one." She bent her neck to one side. "Oh, baby. You been bamboozled. Hoodwinked. Can I hold you?"

Lizzie took a deep breath and straightened. "Not yet. I have to get through the evening."

Willamina offered, "I can make him sick."

Lizzie said, "I prefer doing that myself."

Willamina nodded. "I don't doubt that at all."

Lizzie didn't feel as confident as she sounded. She didn't want to make him sick. A queasy feeling invaded her stomach. Before she could even decide what to think or say or do, she heard voices.

He'd said she was a natural actor.

Maybe she should change into a pirate outfit and get into character. Complete with a sword. A real one. A machete?

She wasn't good at acting like…herself. She really wasn't sure she even knew herself.

Oh, dear. She had to warn Paul. She quickly went out back and told him while Noah and Henri listened.

Paul's eyes glazed over as his face hardened and his hands formed fists.

"Breathe," she said, trying to continue doing that herself. "I'm a big girl. Let me handle it."

The mumbling men followed her and she stopped at the dining room doorway. There stood an unreasonable facsimile of her pastor. This one's hair was not so conservatively cut now, but longer and windblown. Charming dimples were adorable in his handsome smiling face. Long lashes enhanced dreamy dark brown eyes with golden gleams.

He wore a light suit coat over a tangerine, button-down shirt, open at the neck, reminding her of the kind Annabelle bought for Symon. An Alexander Julian, she thought. Of the finest European and Asian fabrics. She couldn't see if he wore suspenders, and she didn't intend to get close enough to find out, but the thought occurred that she'd like to snap them against his chest. Forcefully.

Lizzie walked into the dining room, and he looked her way. After the noise his vocal cords made, a sort of guttural choke, he froze. His entire being registered surprise.

Then his glance shifted to Paul, whose hand rested on her back as if to steady her, and his expression turned to fear.

One didn't have to be a fashion expert to know that a paling, greenish face didn't go well with a tangerine shirt.

The entire group appeared stunned and uncomfortable, but Symon, who apparently had already introduced the others said, "Lizzie, I'd like you to meet Zachary Grant—"

"We—we've met," he said as the words were leaving Symon's mouth.

"I beg your pardon," Lizzie contradicted staunchly. "I've never met a Zachary Grant in my entire life."

Chapter 13

Zach had heard that when people are dying, their life flashes before their eyes. Like a fast-forwarding movie, he supposed. His actions, words, lack of them and intentions over the past week were getting all tangled up, and he figured if he opened his mouth, his tongue would do the same.

He had no script for this.

He knew a bad scene when he saw it. What had seemed to be the big chance of his life just went down the tube. This was no box-office hit. It was a bomb.

Somewhere in the muddle, DeBerry continued to introduce the three men, including Paul. Zach had enough sense not to extend his hand. That would be suicide. Focusing on Paul he said, "I—I guess my name is mud."

By now the others knew disaster was in the air. The special effects were tremendous. "Afraid not," DeBerry said. "Mudd is my dog's name."

Paul, with the same look in his eyes from twenty years ago—a look that clearly said that anybody who hurt his sister would answer to him—now said, "That metaphor is inadequate."

Zach didn't have to ask what he meant. Paul didn't have to say his name wasn't mud. It was dead meat. And that extended beyond his name to his entire existence. These friends of Elizabeth Marshall would not be his stepping stone to success. They would be the rock to his demise.

Since the air had frozen and tension was thick enough to cut with a knife, he thought, had his shoes not turned to superglue on the floor, he should turn, walk out and drive away. But DeBerry had picked him up at the B and B. However, if his feet obeyed, a fast run might do him good, but the men would probably catch him and beat the slop out of him, so his best bet was to try to face...not the music... but the inevitable.

"Is there something we need to talk about?" said the poised, aristocratic, mature woman who had been introduced as Miss B.

But maybe this was just a misunderstanding. Maybe he could straighten it out. "I need to explain." As soon as that word left his mouth, he remembered having told the fiery pirate lady, now an ice maiden, that he would explain. He should have chosen a different word. Maybe a different life.

Comedy was definitely out. Tragedy reigned supreme. Lizzie turned to Paul, now right beside her, and took his arm. She smiled up at him. "The aroma coming from the kitchen is getting to me, Paul. Like some of those dishes you create."

Paul's glance at her, then at Zach again, seemed to say he was waiting for just the right time to deliver his lines. There was no doubt she was the heroine in this story, and Zach the villain, even if they didn't know the entire plot.

Lizzie had become the star of this show, not him. The last lines weren't yet delivered. On second thought, maybe they had already been delivered. The ones that said she'd never met Zachary Grant in her life. The words left unspoken permeated the room.

The elegant Miss B spoke politely. "Yes, let's get our plates and fill them from the sideboard. But first," she said as if nothing amiss had occurred, "Let's bow our heads and I will offer the prayer."

Prayer.

Zach grimaced.

All over. Any chance he had with DeBerry or Lizzie was over before it had gotten started. He squeezed his eyes partially shut while halfway hearing Miss B thank her Lord for the opportunity for them to share their Paris, Hawaii and Savannah experiences with one another. His eyelids went to half-mast when she thanked God for sending Zachary Grant to share with them and asked, "God, fulfill Your purpose in this man."

He glanced at Lizzie whose eyes were closed. Was she thinking of the times when she'd said the prayer when they were together? A glance at Paul revealed his eyes were focused on him. But his face was closed to any emotion.

Miss B ended her prayer with, "Help us relate like Your children, Lord, and serve You always in our words, thoughts and actions."

At the end, Paul echoed her "Amen" more forcefully than the others.

"All right," Miss B said, "Zachary, you may sit here." Her graceful hand, with fingers boasting impressive rings, moved toward the chair at the right of the setting at the head of the table. She picked up her plate, so he did also, aware of the silence. Others did the same.

The men hung back, allowing the women to go first. Zach saw the questioning glances the other two gorgeous women gave Lizzie, and he thought he heard her whisper, "Later."

Zach wondered if he could have handled her anger better than her obvious resolve that she didn't know him and didn't care to. But these were reasonable people. Maybe it wasn't all that bad. He'd just let a misunderstanding go too far.

But if and when they questioned the reason he let it go so far, the answer was obvious—it appeared he was using her to try and get to DeBerry. But that had changed. He had felt badly, and wanted to find the right time to reveal his identity, but that time hadn't come.

And he was here at DeBerry's invitation. DeBerry had sought *him* out. If he could find the right words, this could be smoothed over. He would try to make a decent impression at dinner, let them know he was willing to produce the pirate movie. Yes, he had something to offer. Even a role to the pirate lady. After all, DeBerry's other movie deal had fallen through.

He had to put this into perspective. The misunderstanding was between him and Lizzie, not the others. Sure, they were all protective of her, especially her brother, and that's how it should be. He just needed to act like…no, not act…just be a producer with something to offer and…be… respectful and businesslike.

Symon gestured for Zach to go ahead toward the sidebar, and conversation began about the aroma and taste of the food. A sudden sense of déjà vu, like the one he had experienced when coming up the long driveway with Symon and seeing the big mansion, startled him. He'd been here before, getting punch for a little girl who'd been hurt. Was this…the same place?

He needed to calm his mind and stop imagining. Everybody knew something was amiss between him and Lizzie. But she hadn't reacted with anger. All would be well.

Just then he heard something else familiar.

"If you 'spect to eat, some big strong person, man or woman, better help me with this pot of redeye gravy."

Zach wasn't surprised when Paul immediately headed to the kitchen.

He brought in the pot and set it on the sideboard. Right behind him was Willamina with a huge bowl of green salad. Zach's heart sank. He'd been right in his earlier assessment. She'd know everything about everybody and you just didn't cross a person like that.

Miss B introduced him to Willamina who gave him her hands-on-hips stance and sassy look. "I've done met this Hollywood fellow. Washed his breakfast dishes. Changed his dirty sheets. Talked to him about living water, but don't think it sank in."

Everybody just kept filling their plates, as though nothing unusual was said or done, kind of like with him and Lizzie. Perhaps this was that calm before the storm?

Willamina's eyes were big and round, and she wore a satisfied expression on her face. "I just can't wait to eavesdrop on the conversations at this table tonight. Hmm, uh, mmm-mmm-mmm. It's going to be better than my chicken-fried steak. Well, maybe not that good, but at least close." She turned and disappeared into the kitchen.

Zach could already feel the heat of being fried. Perhaps in hot oil.

Had he been mistaken about DeBerry seeking him out because of filmmaking? Neither Lizzie nor Willamina seemed surprised at his being there.

Did they all know he'd pretended with this beautiful girl?

He doubted they'd use the word *pretended*. Maybe… deceived? Duped? Connived? Schemed? Lied to? He hadn't tried to seduce her but he had thought of it.

Were they all…acting?

* * *

Lizzie thought of the saying about killing someone with kindness. But that is not what Aunt B did. She was the gracious refined Southern lady in charge of this house and this situation. If Lizzie issued a polite request that an unwanted visitor should leave, Aunt B would comply.

But more than that, she would adhere to her religious background and her obedience to what she believed the Lord expected of her. Her spiritual wisdom was a great comfort and help to each of them sitting at the table.

Aunt B had allowed this guest into her home because Symon had asked. Now, aware as everyone else that Lizzie was as aloof as the guest was uncomfortable, Aunt B still offered him the seat of honor on her right at the table.

Aunt B could very well kill another with kindness—although that wouldn't be her intent—much more effectively than any number of foul words or amount of expressed anger.

But Lizzie wasn't angry. She tried to examine her feelings, and felt sorry for Zach because she knew, even without having to look into the eyes of her friends, she had their support.

At other times, two single people near the same age would likely be seated near each other to get better acquainted. But the poignant awareness in the room led Aunt B to make no suggestions other than that Symon might sit across from his guest. She did not suggest that Lizzie be seated next to the man, apparently knowing that could cause an embarrassing scene.

Annabelle sat at Symon's left. Paul pulled out the chair for Lizzie next to Annabelle and he took the chair beside her. Noah looked across at Lizzie with a poignant gaze as if to say his beloved new wife wasn't about to sit next to the person who had spent time with Lizzie and pretended to be a clergyman.

As if sensing the hesitation, Henri said, "I'll just sit here by our guest if that's all right." He probably figured since Aunt B was polite and gracious he should follow the example of his intended. Noah pulled out a chair for Megan and he sat between her and Henri.

Megan tilted her head and wrinkled her brow in silent questioning. Lizzie smiled and hoped the slow blink of her eyes meant all was well. She'd often been called the life of a party, the quick-witted one who made others laugh. That wouldn't happen this evening. Maybe never again. She shrugged one shoulder and turned her face in the direction of a tangerine shirt.

Aunt B was saying, "Zachary Grant. Why don't you go first and tell us a little about yourself."

Lizzie wondered what he'd say. Which self would he reveal? She doubted he'd been excommunicated from the church and turned producer overnight. The fact that he took time replying indicated he, too, wondered what to say.

Finally, he said, "I spent my early years in Savannah. My dad took me to California when I was twelve. He was an actor, now a film director."

"Grant," Aunt B said reflectively. "Was your mother a Brandley before she married your dad?"

"Yes. She was."

Lizzie knew why he looked uncomfortable about that. Then it was worse when Willamina turned from having placed more mouthwatering mashed potatoes on the sideboard. "You know, B. She's now married to that doctor she worked for."

"Dr. Scroff, I believe," Aunt B said.

Zach looked from Willamina to Aunt B. "You know my parents then?"

"Not socially," she said. "Although I married your mother's cousin. That marriage ended after a few years."

"My parents' marriage ended a couple days after your

wedding," Zach said, then scoffed lightly as if he hadn't meant to reveal that. He took a deep breath. "Sorry about getting too personal."

"Quite all right," Aunt B said. "We do that here."

Lizzie was thinking he hadn't talked very personally with her...except about that time in his life. At least *that* didn't seem to be an act. Then his next words were a surprise. "I was at the wedding, and I think the reception was here."

"Yes." Aunt B picked up her glass and took a sip of tea, seeming to think about that.

He was here? Lizzie had been, too. She'd been very young. Kindergarten age. But something was beginning to come to mind. The slow turn of Annabelle's face to hers and her studied look confirmed a memory.

While Aunt B was saying something about several children having been there, some of Julian Brandley's family she hadn't known, some her senator father had invited, Annabelle whispered, "One of the meanies."

Lizzie almost laughed. She hadn't thought of that word in years. A kindergarten word. Glancing across the table she saw Megan grimace, signaling she needed to know what was going on. All Lizzie could do was nod. The explanation had to wait.

Honesty was allowed, but not impoliteness at Aunt B's table. Lizzie was trying to remember which meanie he had been. They'd figure it out later. But now she was aware that his childhood experience hadn't been a fictitious one from Preston Bartholomew. It had been Zachary Grant's childhood, and his devastation over his parents' breakup.

But that did not excuse his pretense. She wasn't sure what the adult word was for a meanie. Was he the one who pushed the boy who spilled punch on her new dress? Or...

Symon drew her attention. "You may not know this. Zach is an actor and producer. He just won a top award at the film festival for a documentary he produced." He focused his remarks to Zach again. "It's actually my agent who informed me you were from Savannah. That interested me and from there I admit, I checked you out on the internet."

Zach nodded. "That's how it's done."

"Well, tell us about your documentary," Aunt B said, and he related an interesting tale about the earthquakes in California. Lizzie thought of how everything could seem so real, so normal, while beneath the surface there was instability. Without warning, the earth could crack, things could break, the world as you knew it…gone.

You learn not to trust in the illusion that all is well. So quickly, that sense of stability changes. Like with her parents' deaths. Aunt B's marriage. Zach's family breakup. The others at the table had experienced the unexpected. One must not put their faith in the fragility of another person or thing.

Finally, Megan and Noah were telling about the Hawaiian islands, luaus, beaches with sand colored white, tan, black and even green. The volcano they flew over. The cool breezes, extraordinary flowers, lush foliage, waterfalls.

Aunt B said she wouldn't go into detail since there was so much to tell about Henri's villa and Paris. She would save that for another time. She held out her hand, displaying her ring. "This sums it up."

Henri added a few comments, but he had been quiet, just looking around at the others, having picked up on the lack of usual joviality in the group. At Paul's turn to share, he said blandly that he, too, would save his stories for later.

"Hmm, uh, mmm-mmm-mmm," preceded Willamina coming in with a big platter. "All that sounded pretty good. But you know we save the best 'til last."

Lizzie figured she wasn't talking about dessert but the fact that the table discussion wasn't over. However, she continued with an explanation of the cake. "This is an accidental cake," she said, and went into the history of it. A cook had reversed some ingredients, which made the outside fully cooked and the inside deliciously different. "You just never know how things might turn out," she said. "A devastating accident or something deliciously gooey and buttery."

"So what have you been up to, Willamina?" Aunt B said, rising, and the others followed to partake of the cake.

Willamina sighed. "I felt as if I was on vacation, just cooking breakfast at the B and B and coming in once a week to take care of my Lizzie. So, I've decided next time anybody goes to Paris or Hawaii, I'm taking them up on going along."

"It's about time," Aunt B said. "It looks as if the next trip might be my and Henri's honeymoon."

Henri gave Willamina a skeptical look.

"Judging by the way he's acting," Willamina said, "looks as if somebody needs to go along and do the cooking."

"You better bring your husband with you, *ma chérie*," Henri said.

"Don't go calling me 'your cherry.' And if I take my husband, I'll have to take the recliner, too." She heaved another big sigh and placed a piece of cake onto a dessert plate. "Need to make sure this cake had the right kind of accident."

Willamina went to the kitchen and the others returned to the table. Aunt B gave them all time to sample the cake and express their delight before she said the expected.

"Lizzie, it's your turn. Other than working and taking care of Mudd and SweetiePie and enduring the edge of that hurricane we heard about, what did you do?"

What to say? She knew they would wait as long as it

took for her to decide how to answer, and explain the difficult situation they all found themselves in.

Should she make a snide remark? Oh, that would be easy. Maybe learn and grow and someday become as gracious and caring as Aunt B? That would take a long, long time. Aunt B had said life's a journey. The spiritual life is not like rising and falling along a straight line. It's like rising and falling and rising again while climbing a mountain.

How easy it would be to embarrass Zach further. To reveal what some of them already knew, and the reason for the tension others were wondering about.

Could she be honest without being vindictive and impolite? She would probably fail miserably. But she would try. She had nothing funny to say. No quips. No jokes. No entertaining stories. What had she done while they were gone? What could she share?

That she was sad, hurt? Is that what she'd done? Become like a drooping pumpkin with a fake smile? Was that Lizzie Marshall?

She looked at Aunt B and saw the love in her eyes. The encouragement. The wisdom of the ages. Like a miracle, the old Lizzie began to return.

She glanced at Paul who eyed her with the expression that it was her call. He'd already laid down his fork and his hand was on his pant leg. She reached over and curved her fingers around his strong hand. Then she looked around the table, even at the reluctant face of Zachary Grant.

Lizzie Marshall laughed lightly, and it wasn't fake. She wouldn't act. "I had a wonderful time," she said. "I met a delightful man. We spent a day at Tybee, seeing the lighthouse, walking the beach, having lunch on Paul's porch. On Sunday we went to church, then rode bikes to the City Market and ate gelato at Café GelatOhhh!!"

She moved her hand away from Paul's. She thought of how Symon had introduced her to Zachary Grant, who had been wise enough not to extend his hand. She wouldn't have taken it. Preston Bartholomew had stolen her heart and her emotions. She hadn't been about to give anyone her hand, too.

"And Symon," she said. Annabelle leaned back so he could see her better. "We talked a lot about *The Pirate's Treasure.*"

"I see," Symon said, as if he were simply making a casual comment.

"He drove your car. I hope that's all right."

"Perfectly. While I was gone, the car was yours."

The silence and tension threatened, and forks seemed to pick around remnants of cake or just on empty plates. Aunt B asked, "Do we know this friend?"

"No," Lizzie said. "He's gone. He won't be back."

"Does he have a name?"

"Oh, yes," and Zachary Grant said it blandly as she proudly proclaimed, "Rev. Dr. Preston Bartholomew."

The sounds Annabelle and Megan made were akin to someone about to lose their dinner. Annabelle's head turned to Lizzie, then she put her hand over her open mouth. Megan's eyes danced, and she inverted her lips to keep from laughing. They seemed in between chagrin and hilarity. Noah took a deep breath and his shoulders straightened. Henri's dark eyes sympathized and his lips pursed as if he'd like to kiss her hand and console *ma chérie.* Symon looked resigned. Aunt B nodded, as if Lizzie were doing just fine in not behaving like a clichéd, hot-tempered redhead.

Yes, the old Lizzie had returned. She could mask that silly broken heart and it would mend because it wasn't real. She'd fallen for a pastor who didn't exist. She'd fallen for a character, not a person. And wasn't that hilarious?

Wasn't that like the silly, stupid Lizzie? The one who didn't have her head on straight? Surely the humor wasn't lost on anyone. And knowing how quickly laughter could turn to something else if you weren't careful, especially when you were laughing at yourself, she turned her face toward Paul again.

He obviously wasn't entertained.

"I think," Paul said to Zachary Grant, with a voice as resolute as his gaze, "It's time to step outside."

Chapter 14

It flashed through Zach's mind that Lizzie should say *Don't bother, he's not worth it, let it go.* Or Symon would say he should just call a cab and hightail it back to town. Or the lovely lady at the head of the table would say that's enough, everyone should be civil and she'd politely recommend that he please vacate the premises immediately.

They were apparently slow on the uptake. Paul pushed away from the table, stood and positioned the chair forward in a way that meant he wasn't going to the sideboard and returning to the table.

Although Zach's eyes were on Paul, he was aware Lizzie and her two friends were focusing on their dessert plates, unperturbed, as if nothing were amiss. Was that what one called loyal to a fault?

His attention moved to Symon when the author said, "Be right with you. Don't want to miss a crumb of this cake." Sure, Symon wouldn't need an explanation as to why he and Lizzie had discussed the pirate book. Zach's intentions were no doubt by this time like a movie playing across the screen of their minds—a box-office bomb. Or worse, a disaster before it got a good start.

Symon shoved the forkful of cake in his mouth, licked his lips and took a swallow of coffee. He stood. Okay, two against one. Nope, wrong again. Noah was getting up. But maybe he'd stop them from beating him too badly.

"Henri," Miss B said in her genteel way, and Zach glanced over at her. Perhaps she would consider Zach a relative, however distant. On second thought, she was divorced from his mother's cousin whose reputation wasn't all that commendable.

Miss B looked past him at her fiancé. "You haven't seen our young men in this kind of action, have you? Perhaps you should join them."

"Mais oui, avec plaisir." He stood, giving the appearance of one enjoying the pleasure he just expressed. He'd be a great character in a movie. Too bad Zach wouldn't be around to film one anymore, since four fit men were taking him…out back.

Willamina appeared. "If you need some sweet tea out there later on, just holler."

Zach had a feeling any hollering wouldn't be for tea. Not from him anyway. Paul headed for the dining room doorway, followed by Noah. Zach rose from his chair.

"Mudd. SweetiePie," Symon said. "Come."

They did. Apparently the animals would be in on it, too. What a shame to have chicken-fried steak and accidental cake knocked out of him. The dog and cat could lick up the small pieces.

He followed the men out to the patio. They gathered around one of the white wrought-iron tables shaded by an umbrella. Symon pulled over a chair from another table. Zach wondered if they each would hit him with a chair or would they sit.

They sat, as if they were just a few men enjoying a cool evening, the soft breeze stirring the moss swaying from the trees. The evening sun lazed above them, slowly painting the sky with cool blue, gray and white. The South, or at least Savannah, had a fragrance, and the rapid rise and fall of his chest indicated he was breathing deeply of it. His heart was also getting a workout.

This patio, these tables, stirred the memory of the wedding where his heart had been broken, his world shattered, his life disrupted. That scene had been filled with action, voices, fighting, a hurt little girl, Paul's threat.

Now, the quiet was stifling. Why didn't someone hit him? Curse him? Threaten him? The emotions of decades ago rose up in him and he felt as if the men had already beaten him.

He looked over at Paul. "We were out here about twenty years ago."

Paul nodded. "I know." His nostrils flared slightly with his intake of breath. "My sister was too little to take care of herself back then."

Zach dared say, "If I recall, she did all right."

"No," he said. "She hadn't learned that fighting isn't the way to settle things."

Disappointment washed over him. He had the feeling he'd be better off if they hit him and sent him on his way. What did they have in mind?

"Lizzie can pretty much take care of herself now," Paul said. "She can handle things in her own way. Whether or not she wants you to answer to her is her decision. However," he said with a meaningful stare. "She's still my sister. And that part is my affair."

This was Paul's turn. He needed to speak his mind and Zach knew he must be quiet and listen if he valued his teeth.

Paul placed his forearms on the table and leaned forward. "You were with my sister in my restaurant, not once but twice. At Tybee. At my home. Ate my food. That in itself is fine. Except you did it under false pretenses. Used a fake identity of being a pastor, of all things. Sounds underhanded to me. When someone conceals their identity, the impression given is not a favorable one."

Zach would like to say what he told himself at the beginning. He hadn't pretended to be a pastor. He'd been mistaken as one. The charade had been fun, like Lizzie pretending to be a pirate. That's all. Nothing underhanded. That he was waiting for the right time to say he was Zachary Grant.

He opened his mouth to explain, then he promptly closed it.

"I didn't have you come out here for a fist fight," Paul said. "But to give you an opportunity to explain."

"You're my guest," Symon said. "I brought you here as a friendly gesture, but it has caused tension. I would like an explanation but if you don't want to give it, I can take you back to the B and B."

"Incidentally," Noah said. "My wife owns the B and B."

Well, Zach was thinking, *there's always a hotel.* He looked at Henri, wondering if he had anything to add, maybe suggest he go to Paris and jump off the Eiffel Tower. But Henri moved the finger away that had been resting on his lips. "They're about truth around here, son," he said. "Amazing what that can do for a fellow. It got me the woman I'm going to marry." He angled his head toward the house as if indicating Miss B.

Truth?

He'd rather they beat him up and leave him bleeding. He could justify it, like he had to himself all along. But he remembered when they sat at the dining room table. Lizzie had said they discussed the pirate book and DeBerry had said, "I see."

They all saw…enough.

He exhaled a deep breath. "Right after filming the pastor scene, without taking time to change, I went to the Pirate's Cave to see the setting that inspired your book." DeBerry didn't appear surprised. "Then the pirate lady revealed that the movie deal had fallen through."

DeBerry gave a nod as if knowing what was coming.

He might as well say the words. "My natural instinct was to…use her…for more information. I am sorry," he said, looking at Symon. "I was thinking like I would at the film festival. You make contacts. Things happen because of who you know and being in the right place at the right time."

He looked at Paul. "The second night I found out you were her brother and I remembered your threat twenty years ago and didn't think the Cave was the place to continue our talk, so I suggested Tybee. I planned to tell her my real name before we left." His breathing was shallow. "But she drove up in that black sports car and said it belonged to DeBerry. The producer—" he pointed to his chest "—chose to continue the deception longer. Then at Tybee—" he let out a breath "—she became…Lizzie."

"Meaning?" Paul said immediately.

"The pastor chose Lizzie."

"But the pastor isn't real," Paul said.

"No," Zach agreed. "But it became obvious Lizzie wouldn't appreciate my little charade, my joke. She liked the kind of man a pastor should be. I acted…I acted, well, as a clergyman. But it's a far cry from who I am."

"Who are you?" Paul asked.

The question startled Zach. He'd never heard it asked quite like that. Someone might ask what do you do? Where are you from? But…who? He didn't consider himself such a far cry from anybody else. He had his faults and his good points. What did Paul want to hear? That he was a scoundrel and a fool? That went without saying. He spoke tentatively. "Basically, an actor and producer."

"That's your job," Paul said.

Silence ensued and he couldn't read their deadpan expressions. "I'm not sure what you want me to say. I mean, how would you answer that?"

"For starters," Paul said, "what were your intentions with my sister?"

"To get her to like me enough—"

"Enough?"

Zach nodded. "Enough to introduce me to Sy DeBerry."

"So you weren't interested in her personally?" Paul's tone had an ironic ring to it. What guy wouldn't be interested in her?

How in the world was he to answer that question to a protective big brother? He shifted the position of his legs and picked at the table a moment. He thought a bit of amusement played in the eyes of everyone but Paul. He took a deep breath. "I thought she was the most delightful pirate I'd ever seen."

Okay, how to be truthful. "The more I saw of her, the more I regretted having fooled her. I knew she liked Preston Bartholomew so I continued to act like I thought he would." He spoke to the table. Or was it to himself? "I knew she wouldn't be impressed with me, and I couldn't seem to find the right time to say I wasn't Preston Bartholomew."

With a glance out to the yard, the green grass, the tables, the trees, his emotions traveled back twenty years. Why not take it all the way? They wanted truth. He didn't, but it raised its ugly head. "The thought of telling her made me feel like a twelve-year-old again, when I thought my parents didn't like me enough to keep being my parents." He tried to laugh, but the sound was strange. "She wouldn't like me enough..." He shrugged, and his fingers grasped his legs as if they planned to go somewhere. Run away? Hide?

Zach wanted to say he should just leave. But he wasn't sure if they would let him go. Four against one wasn't exactly the best of odds.

Chapter 15

"Well, Lizzie. What do you think of Zachary Grant?" Aunt B asked after the men went out into the backyard.

She slapped her hands onto the table. "Like I said, I never met a Zachary Grant in my life. I don't know him."

Annabelle grinned. "You and he have a lot in common."

"Ach!" Lizzie screeched. "You mean I'm a great pretender. One who misrepresents herself, lies, the biggest kind of hypocrite, meets somebody and—" She closed her eyes and her mouth at that.

Megan picked up on it. "And what? Falls for him?"

Lizzie puffed out a sigh and flashed arrows with her eyes. "No. I mean, yes." Shaking her head, she hedged. "I didn't fall for Zach. I was with the Rev. Dr. Preston Bartholomew. I was very restrained, respectful, being the kind of friend a visiting pastor would appreciate."

Lizzie pushed away from the table and stood. She pulled on a lock of her hair. "I'm trying very hard not to act like a stereotypical redhead and...and...throw something."

A deep breath raised her shoulders and she breathed out heavily.

Megan giggled. "There's only one reason you're so disturbed."

Annabelle tsked her tongue. "You always told us about our clicking with Symon and Noah. Well, honey, you click with Zach."

Shaking her head in denial, Lizzie said, "No. It's the character I fell for."

"He's still Zach," Megan said.

"No, he's not Zach. He doesn't exist. I fell for a pastor character, of all things. And what makes it worse is that he let me know he was unavailable. I mean, it's like… like…falling for Leonardo DeCaprio because he's Jack in the *Titanic* movie. It's not the person, it's the character, and you know it's fantasy. You're Rose and that's why you love Jack."

"Well…" Megan said, "Can Veronica love Preston? And transfer that to Lizzie and Zach?"

"Not a chance. I couldn't be the real me and he wasn't the real him."

"You can't be anybody but you," Annabelle said.

Lizzie shook her head. "I had to downplay me. Be more reserved. If I hadn't made that vow about dating, and Preston Bartholomew hadn't said he was a man totally dedicated to his career, which I thought was the church, I would have tried to make him dedicated to me. That's the one thing I can't toy with. You don't try and come between someone and his faith. But…" She held her head and sighed. This was a puzzle too difficult to piece together. "I don't know if he has any faith. He made me do the praying when we ate together."

"So you were acting, too?" Annabelle said and Lizzie knew that was a rhetorical question.

"Not in the same way he was." With pleading eyes she looked at Aunt B. "It's not the same, is it?"

"Of course not," Aunt B said. "Different sides of our personalities are revealed according to those we're relating to. We may act childish when relating to a child. Our focus is on faith when comforting a troubled person. We're reserved around some, and open around others. When Henri and I began to relate as adults I was more reserved, perhaps like you mean about your being with Preston Bartholomew." She smiled. "But Zachary Grant was still in there."

"But who is he?"

Aunt B gave a chuckle. "According to him, he was a young man who acted a part, saw self-advantage in continuing the charade, began to fall for Lizzie and was trapped by his own deceit. He took it too far."

"How should I feel about that?"

"That's your decision," Aunt B said. "You tell us."

Lizzie groaned. "I feel all the rotten things a person is supposed to feel when another person withholds the truth that would make a difference in how you relate to them." She took a deep breath, both liking and disliking the knowing expressions on their faces and in their eyes.

"Okay, here it is. I would love for him to be what he looked like when the hurricane blew him into the Cave. A gorgeous swashbuckler with dancing eyes and dreamy looks *and* be an actor and producer. That appeals to me. We could have had great conversations about movies and actors and characters."

"But you can't now." Megan's lips turned down and Lizzie knew she was acting.

"No." She shook her head. "Because he deliberately misled me."

Annabelle heaved a sigh. "I know. Like Symon when he didn't tell me he was a famous novelist but wanted me to like or dislike him as the caretaker's son and not for his success."

"And just look at my life," Megan said with a shake of her head. "Noah spied on me so he could tell my runaway boyfriend how I was getting along. Then he pretended not to love me. Oh…men."

Lizzie couldn't help but laugh. Her precious friends had worked out their problems and were now happily married. "But that's different," she insisted. "He deliberately tried to use me."

"And of course you can never forgive him for that," Aunt B said.

Quiet pervaded the room. Her statement was one for contemplation. Lizzie nodded. "That's something that came up in our conversation. He asked me what's the point of forgiveness if you still have to pay the consequences?"

Megan was quick on the uptake. "How did you answer?"

"I didn't," she said, remembering. "Now I think he really wanted an answer. In all these years, he hasn't forgiven his mother for the breakup of their family."

Willamina turned from the sidebar she was cleaning off. "From what I heard, she was all broke up about her boy going to live with his dad in California. But they gave him the choice. Lot of bad things have been said about her for that."

"I can't fault her," Aunt B said. "That would have to have been hard."

They all looked at her with understanding, knowing she would be thinking of the son she had to give up when she was sixteen.

After a brief moment, Annabelle said, "So it was Zach asking about forgiveness, and not the actor."

"When he asked, I thought he was testing my theology. I wanted to think about it instead of just saying it has eternal consequences." She sat again and looked at Aunt B. "Paul said that sounded like an Aunt B question."

"Oh, my." Aunt B's eyes brightened with anticipation. "Looks as if we need to have that Zachary Grant over for another dinner. At least a meeting."

Willamina chuckled. "Last time I looked out the window he seemed to be getting a good dose of that living water. Wonder if he's gonna drown or get washed clean." She shook her head. "Who knows about them Hollywood fellows?"

Lizzie didn't. She recalled Symon having talked about the cliché "You can't tell a book by its cover." You could get an impression from it, but it doesn't tell you the whole story.

She liked Zachary Grant's cover. She had only an inkling of his story.

"Have you learned from this?" Aunt B asked.

"I'm learning," Lizzie said. "I really like the idea of his being an actor and producer. I love the way he treated me. But he was acting a part so I could help him get to Symon. That…hurts."

"What a predicament," Annabelle said. "What would you want the real Zach to have done?"

Lizzie moaned. She would like for him to have swept her into his arms, kissed her lips and then declare his undying love for her. Sighing, she looked up at the ceiling. "Lord, forgive me."

Her friends giggled. Right now, they weren't any help at all. She shook her head. "Yes, I've learned. Mr. Perfect… doesn't exist."

"Oh, yes, honey," Willamina said. "He sure does."

"It's getting late," Symon said, and Zach glanced at the graying sky. Symon pushed away from the table, as did the others. Zach followed suit, wondering if this was the end or if more punches would be thrown, physical this time. He'd welcome those. Soul-searching had never been up his alley and he wasn't too fond of it now.

"I'd like to…" *Be truthful.* "I…should…apologize to the women. You think they'll want me back in the house?"

"They won't hurt you," Paul said, but the glint in his eyes meant there was no guarantee about Lizzie's brother.

He felt like that twelve-year-old boy again. Hurt, broken, confused. His parents had done it to him back then. This time, he had done it to himself. Messed up the best things that had ever come his way, his career and the most wonderful girl in the world.

He didn't want to hurt Lizzie. "What seemed like a clever joke that Lizzie would laugh about became a deception I didn't know how to get out of."

After considerable quiet, Symon asked, "How long will you be in Savannah?"

I could leave now, he was thinking. "I'd planned to stay a few days after the festival to visit my dad's relatives and friends."

As they walked across the patio, Symon said, "We swim most mornings. Join us?"

Zach glanced around. Symon's eyes remained on him. "Me?"

Symon nodded.

"Good idea," Noah said, and glanced at Paul who said, "Sure."

"Where? What time?"

"Fitness Center," Henri said. "We can ride together since we're both at the B and B."

He tried to read the men's faces but they seemed blank. No anger. Deadpan. They all seemed in agreement. Had they done this before?

Okay, so they weren't through with him yet.

They'd decided to drown him.

Zach entered the house with the men, and everyone but him walked toward their women. Zach didn't have a woman. The gorgeous redhead picked up her crystal goblet of iced tea and brought it to her lips. Lips that would never touch his.

Zach stood at the end of the table, telling himself to act the role of polite man with integrity. And do it quickly. He focused on Miss B. "I'm sorry."

The words sounded choked. He felt as if blood were draining from his face. His hands were clammy.

"In that case," Miss B said gently, "if you're going to be around for a while, let's try again."

What could he say? He had to go through this...or worse... again?

They all walked down the hallway and out onto the front porch, standing for a few minutes until Henri and Miss B came out. "Since I'm driving CoraBeth's car," Henri said and Zach assumed that was Miss B's name, "I can take Zach to the B and B."

"Fine," Symon said.

The author's quick answer seemed to confirm that Symon was no longer considering having Zach adapt his book into a movie.

Annabelle and Symon headed for the cottage. Noah and Megan went to their car, and Henri said he'd meet Zach in the driveway with Miss B's car.

Miss B went inside, while Lizzie stood at the banister with her hands on the white railing. Henri would be bringing the car around at any moment.

Zach wanted to reach out. Touch her. Make her know that nothing in the world was more important than she. "I love..." He saw her stiffen, turn her face away from him, toward the driveway. "I loved every moment with you."

She gazed out over the smooth green lawn, speaking to it, not him. "So did I." Then she faced him. He admired the way the breeze lifted her hair from the side of her face. Her manner was a far cry from the lively pirate lady. "I wanted to see Preston Bartholomew again and say goodbye and wish him well. I'm glad I have this chance." The car driven by Henri appeared in the driveway. "Goodbye."

She didn't extend her hand. If she had, he would have taken it and pulled her to him, crying or begging or doing whatever necessary.

She said she'd never met Zachary Grant in her life.

Now she had. And he had been anything but impressive.

She looked toward Henri and lifted her hand in goodbye. Zach walked down the steps to the path leading to the driveway. When he glanced at the porch, Lizzie opened the screen door and disappeared into the house.

She'd said goodbye to the Rev. Dr. Preston Bartholomew.

Zachary Grant might as well not exist. To her anyway.

And he wasn't too pleased about it himself.

He didn't say goodbye. If there was any way, he'd like to say hello again. Start over.

And if he'd been Preston Bartholomew, that might have been possible.

But he was Zach.

And like Paul had asked, who was that?

Chapter 16

"Uhf, uhf, uhf, uhf, uhf."

With each punch, Lizzie thought about Henri driving Zach to swim at the Fitness Center with him, Paul, Symon and Noah each morning at 6:00 a.m. while the females worked out on the exercise equipment in Aunt B's basement.

Of course she knew their motives. Symon had his reasons for seeking out Zachary Grant in the first place. Paul wanted to show he was a significant presence in his sister's life. They each would let Zach know they didn't stand for any nonsense but weren't going to abuse him. They'd just be examples of men who try to allow the Lord to be first in their lives.

But she didn't fool herself into thinking Zachary Grant could turn into Preston Bartholomew. And he hadn't wanted her in the first place. His intentions had been to get to Sy DeBerry.

"Uhf, uhf, uhf, uhf, uhf."

All of a sudden Lizzie stopped punching the bag. Annabelle and Megan were running on the treadmills but giggling and watching her.

Aunt B, lying on the weight bench, chuckled.

"What?" Lizzie said, between breaths.

Annabelle snickered. "That bag doesn't stand a chance."

"Lost the match totally," Megan added.

Lizzie picked up her towel and wiped her sweaty forehead, then reached for her bottle of water. "Well, what do you think we're down here for?" She unscrewed the top and drank.

"To stay in shape." Megan slowed to a trot. "Not to desecrate the equipment."

Annabelle quipped, "Wonder what she named that punching bag?"

"Now, girls." Aunt B sat up. "We've seen you both give the equipment a real workout."

Lizzie harrumphed. "Right. Not long ago you thought your worlds had collapsed." She plopped down beside Aunt B. "Better be nice. You're going to be needing spinster Aunt Lizzie one of these days when you start having all those babies."

"Oh, you silly girl." Annabelle stepped off the treadmill and unscrewed the top of her water bottle. "Your right one will come along."

"Nope. I've learned my lesson. I really meant that prayer about not trying to find Mr. Perfect. I think Preston Bartholomew was sent to the Cave to show me how I can be distracted by outer appearances. I mean, you gotta admit he's gorgeous. I've learned I need to get to know a person and not judge by first impressions."

Megan stepped off the treadmill. "But you were with him for five days."

"Okay, make that second, third or fourth impressions." She nodded for emphasis.

"He's been swimming with the guys," Annabelle reminded her. "Symon believes Zach is really sorry for concealing his identity too long."

"I'm sure he is," Lizzie said. "He's hurt his chances with Symon by being underhanded about it." She grunted. "It's really ironic that Symon sought him out. So if he's sorry, that's probably what he's sorry about."

Annabelle draped her towel around her neck. "Symon sought him out because of a project he has in mind. But he'd never work with him if he thought he was untrustworthy. Or if you objected."

Lizzie jumped up and tossed her towel into the laundry basket. "If Symon wants to work with him, it doesn't matter to me."

"What does Paul think of him?" Megan asked.

Lizzie huffed. "Paul knows by the arrows my eyes shoot his way that he's not to bring up the conversation about a character I thought was a real person."

They giggled, but their eyes expressed sympathy. Aunt B put her arm around Lizzie's shoulders. "You know we love you, hon."

"Yes, and I've been silly. But this takes the cake, don't you think?"

"Accidental...cake?" Annabelle teased.

"Right," Megan said. "Some things turn out different than you'd expected."

"Did with us," Annabelle said.

Megan pointed her finger at Annabelle. "You planned to marry Wesley instead of Symon." She pointed at herself. "I thought Michael might be the one for me but it turned out to be Noah."

Aunt B stood. "Don't forget me. Never in my life would I have expected to marry Henri Beauvais."

Annabelle punched Lizzie's arm. "See. Never know what yummy stuff's in store for you."

"Oh, I know," Lizzie quipped, heading for the stairs, the others following. "My accidental cake is the kind Willamina makes. I'll just settle for fat and calories." Her tennis shoes trod heavily up the steps. "Mr. Perfect is a fantasy."

Aunt B cleared her throat. "Then you won't mind if we have a family dinner and invite Zachary Grant."

"Who?" Lizzie quipped.

They chuckled and she shook her head as they all entered the kitchen. Lizzie faced them. "I'm supposed to be the one who doesn't know reality from fantasy. But you guys act as if Zachary Grant is Preston Bartholomew. Well FYI, I see a difference. And Zachary Grant has baggage. I don't want a man I have to fix."

"Darlin'," Aunt B drawled. "Nobody can fix another. God is the great fixer and our men are good examples of that."

"Hmm." Lizzie looked around. "Would be nice if Willamina was here to fix our breakfast." Then it occurred to her that Willamina would be fixing Zachary Grant's breakfast at the B and B. Henri's, too. Symon and Noah might join them.

"Which brings me to a subject I'd like us to discuss," Megan said. "I've been thinking about maybe selling the B and B."

"Really?" Lizzie's heart rate accelerated. "I've been wondering what to do. I don't want to move in with Paul. I shouldn't live with Aunt B and Henri after they're married."

"You know that's all right."

"I know. But at some point in my life I need to be out on my own. Owning the B and B might just be perfect." She grimaced at the word *perfect,* and retracted. "I mean, might be the Lord's plan for me."

Now, why did they all just shake their heads?

* * *

Two evenings later, Lizzie had the opportunity to prove there was nothing between her and Zachary Grant. Symon invited them to a low-country boil in his backyard down near the creek.

Lizzie could hardly say she had something else to do when they all knew she could very well do what she pleased.

"I don't like for it to look as if I'm paired up with Zach," she said to Paul.

"It won't," he said. "I can leave the Cave for a couple hours. Symon has some business to discuss and he'd like to include us."

Lizzie wondered if Symon decided Zach might be right to produce his pirate movie. He'd have to think highly of Zach and his work to do that. But that was between him and Zach.

There was nothing…nothing between her and Zach. Except the memory of Preston Bartholomew. But that would pass.

So she joined Annabelle, Megan and Aunt B in the kitchen making double fudge, dark-chocolate brownies and soon the aroma wafting through the open windows from the direction of the cottage gave them all hungry grumbles and moans of anticipation. They took the brownies out of the oven and set them on the kitchen table, then busied themselves with the sweet tea Annabelle had made that afternoon. They filled the drinking glasses with ice and poured the tea.

Henri came in and Lizzie knew that meant Zach was outside.

"I was told to get the sweet tea." He looked charming in his jeans and dark turtleneck. Annabelle handed him the full pitcher and they followed him out with glasses.

They walked out to the clearing to a long wooden table

set beneath tall live oaks. Lizzie's quick glance at Zach registered that he wore jeans and a light tan V-neck sweater over a brown T-shirt. Those colors would complement his eyes. If she happened to look.

He glanced at her and she shifted her gaze to Paul who was stirring the pot hanging over the fire pit while Symon and Noah brought wooden folding chairs from the basement.

"Symon said I should put the glasses on the newspaper so it won't blow away," Henri said, his handsome face skeptical, as if he thought he hadn't heard right. "It's fine, Henri," Aunt B assured him. "This is just part of low-country boil."

"I've never heard of low-country boil." Henri set the glasses on the newspaper Zach was spreading on the table.

"I guess I've always known the term," Zach said, holding down the corner of the paper being lifted by the breeze. Henri set a glass on it. "I know corn on the cob is in it." He looked over his shoulder at Paul. "What else?"

"This is Willamina's recipe. By the way, where is she?"

"Had a church meeting," Aunt B replied.

Paul nodded. "Besides the ears of corn broken in half, we have small red potatoes, crab, Old Bay seasoning, spicy smoked sausage, fresh shrimp and I can't tell you any other spices because Willamina would kill me. It's our secret." He grinned. "And it's not all thrown into the pot at one time. This is a one-pot wonder, but these ingredients take different times to cook."

"Oh, the cocktail sauce," Annabelle exclaimed. "I'll get it." She hurried toward the cottage.

Paul began relating the recipe's history. "Used to be called Frogmore Stew. Richard Gay was a National Guardsman who had to cook a meal for one hundred soldiers and he remembered this family recipe. He was from Frogmore. As it became more popular it began to be called low-country boil. Uh-oh," he said. "Better pray. The shrimp is turning pink."

Henri said the prayer, and by that time Annabelle returned with the containers of cocktail sauce on a tray. Symon set them along the middle of the table.

"Can I do anything?" Zach offered.

"Sure," Paul said. "I have a couple strainers here." Paul dipped down, held it up and let it drain, then handed the strainer to Zach.

Zach stared at it. "You don't mean…?"

"Yep. Pour it out on the newspaper. That's what it's for."

Noah laughed and took the strainer from Zach. "You get the next one."

After Zach saw that Noah dumped the contents of the strainer on the newspaper, he did the same, and went back for more.

"We men know how to serve up dinner," Paul said. "Makes cleanup easier."

"This is a common practice," Aunt B said to Henri, who looked more skeptical than Zach.

Lizzie decided to put in her two cents' worth. "If a palmetto bug drops into it from the trees, don't worry. That's just protein."

They were all laughing, having fun, and she thought Zach behaved much like Preston Bartholomew would have. Kind, pleasant, fun and he seemed to fit in, except he made it difficult for her to feel completely natural and relaxed. She'd never before let a man control her emotions. But that was because he reminded her of Preston Bartholomew… who didn't exist.

Now, how was a person supposed to deal with that?

When Zach went back for the last strainer full he stopped. "Do you know the cat and dog are in the creek?"

They all simply laughed, but as soon as everyone took their seats, the conversation turned to a story that had been told many times. Zach was the only one who hadn't heard it.

"SweetiePie and Mudd became friends in that creek the same day Annabelle fell in and Symon caught her," Aunt B said.

Symon moved a crab leg from his lips. "Yes, that's the day I kissed her, and then she kissed me. Better than low-country boil. Although this is a close second."

Annabelle playfully punched his arm, and they shared those loving looks Lizzie had so longed for.

Megan then explained that she'd wanted a special kiss. Noah said, "So the first one was on the pink sand of Eleuthra when we were on a mission trip."

Megan grinned. "And the one in the gazebo at Forsythe Park was rather memorable."

"Rather memorable? That's what led us to a honeymoon in Hawaii."

"Well, now," Aunt B said. "My engagement kiss was in a sidewalk café in Paris."

"You notice she didn't say 'first kiss,'" Lizzie quipped. She clicked her tongue. "You kissed in public?"

"Well, you can't accept an engagement ring and just sit there and admire the finger."

Henri laughed. "Right on the mouth. A bear hug included. And we got a standing ovation."

Lizzie laughed with them and dared not look at Zachary Grant. Sure, she'd been kissed. But not like they meant. Hers had been a meeting of the lips. Not unpleasant. In fact, she had liked it. But there hadn't been that "many splendored thing" that rocked her world.

Zach didn't seem any more eager than she to discuss if and where and when and with whom they'd been, or not, been kissed. Lizzie refused to look at his lips, and forced her thoughts away from being in the tunnel … and his finger touching her mouth when he had adjusted her mustache. If he thought of her lips at all, he'd...laugh.

The light breeze stirred the moss hanging from the trees. The sounds of chewing, finger licking, glasses clinking and ice tinkling all mingled together.

Symon didn't ask Paul, but directed a grin at him.

Paul lifted a hand. "Not telling my secrets. But I'll say this. These women are fascinating. I love them all. But a young woman has never appealed to me in a serious, personal way. I'm waiting for a mature one. If that happens, fine. If not, I'll enjoy being a bachelor."

Lizzie had never heard him say anything like that. She realized she was staring at him when he faced her and winked. "Don't think too hard," he said.

"Sounds like a plot for a book," Symon commented.

Lizzie thought so, too. The enigmatic grin on Paul's face indicated as much, but he was as silent as she was normally vocal.

Soon they discussed movies they'd seen and liked or didn't like. After they cleaned off the table and cleared the yard, they went inside to the cottage kitchen for brownies and coffee.

Symon directed a statement to Zach. "My agent says you're being considered for the lead in *Loving Life.*"

Zach nodded. "So are a couple others, including Mario Victoro."

Lizzie tried to keep her cool. Mario Victoro? The Adonis of the universe?

She dared not look at Annabelle or Megan because she knew their eyes and brows would be doing the bunny hop and their hearts would be pounding out of their chests.

Just like hers.

No, Zachary Grant was in no way Rev. Dr. Preston Bartholomew.

Chapter 17

"Zach," Symon said. "I never did get around to telling you how I knew about you."

Zach continued to chew the brownie, the second most delightful presence in the room—next to Lizzie—and shot him a quizzical look.

He'd wondered at first what the men were doing with him, inviting him to go swimming and hang out with them. And he and Henri had done a few things together since they were both staying at the B and B.

After a day or so, Zach understood they weren't after his hide, but were showing him what friendly, decent men were like.

"My agent told me about your documentary, and I was able to view it. I like your work."

"Thank you," Zach said as calmly as he could, despite the anticipation of possibly acting in, or even producing, Symon's movie.

He pinched off a small piece of brownie and popped it

into his mouth. Small, so he wouldn't choke on his excitement, and he tried to keep his expression bland.

Symon began to explain his project. "The university where I'm writer-in-residence is interested in a promo video about our program. That I'm fine with," he said, "but I'm thinking how I can go further, perhaps a documentary to promote both the program and the seminar I'm planning for next spring."

Zach picked up his cup and gulped some coffee, needing a moment to get his mind off a movie and focus it on where his expertise lay. He set his cup down. "What do you have in mind?"

"A media arts seminar led by professionals, which shows how TV, music, film, acting, screenwriting and marketing all work together."

Zach nodded, understanding that each arts discipline had its own focus, but there was a definite crossover. And value in combining expertise. "Do you have faculty in mind?"

"I want to involve as many Savannah and Southern artists who have achieved success as I can. Like your dad, for instance. And you, who have an award-winning documentary."

"Only one award," Zach said.

"How many does it take?"

Zach laughed. "Okay. Thanks."

He liked this. Very much. "I see the value. The different media arts are separate most of the time. Would be great to bring them together."

"I already have top professionals in their fields wanting to participate. I'd like to use the family analogy on the film or DVD, showing how we work separately, yet together, and the bigger arts professions can do that."

"Tell me," Zach said, getting excited about it.

"It's only in the idea stage, so I'm still sorting things

out," Symon said, making Zach realize a world-famous novelist had his insecurities, too. "Something like we do here. We each have our own expertise, but we get together—like we're doing now—to talk about what each one is doing and offer our ideas or just be supportive."

"Like what?" Zach wanted to know. "Don't tell me about yourself, but expound the abilities and jobs of those here at the table. Just bear with me."

"Somebody made great brownies," Noah said, and several people laughed as hands reached toward the platter.

"Noah has a renovation and construction company," Symon said. "This kitchen is a result of his talent."

"Oh, he's a great prayer," Megan said. "He always starts our sessions that way."

"Megan is into history and interior design."

"Lizzie acts and is a natural storyteller."

"Annabelle models and sings. She writes children's books and Megan illustrates."

"Aunt B is a teacher who critiques, edits and advises."

"Paul and Willamina are the food experts."

"Henri…" Zach said. "What do you do, Henri?"

"I know." Lizzie waved her hand. "He kisses hands and speaks French."

"True." He kissed his fingertip and sent it her way. He looked affectionately at Lizzie, something Zach envied. "But I could throw in a little description of a romantic villa, the Eiffel Tower and—" he grinned at Miss B "—sidewalk cafés. And I've been a pediatrician for a few decades."

Nobody said the most obvious, that Symon was the famous novelist. Then he spoke up. "I grew up as the caretaker's son," he said. "I know about landscaping and basic upkeep of property and homes."

"What you just did," Zach said, "is show what can be accomplished by a family working together."

Symon was nodding. "That's what I want to do with

the arts idea. Use the documentary to show how different genres come together."

"Use the analogy of a family to show what can be done with those in the arts cooperating. You're a family here," Zach said. "The closest I've ever known. The documentary could show both. One, this family working together. Two, those in the arts working together. Maybe your writing students could come up with scenes and have your actors perform it."

Symon liked it. "Yes, family analogy enhancing each other's abilities will enable the viewers to see the same thing can happen with the media arts family."

"Oh, I know," Lizzie said. "At the seminar you could have a murder mystery for attendees to solve. Some write it. Some act. Others solve. It's filmed."

"The Cave would be the perfect place for that," Zach said, feeling as if he were in his element now. Maybe it was time to show he recognized talent. The light inside Lizzie had turned on, and it shone, warming him.

He ventured to ask, "Lizzie, have you thought about acting professionally?"

"I've been asked that many times, most often during the film festival."

Ah, others had discovered her before he did. Of course they would have.

She laughed. "Not in movies."

"Perhaps you should."

"Why?"

Why?

She looked and sounded serious with that one word. That turned the question back to him. Why did he want to produce DeBerry's story? Yes, for self-serving reasons. It was his profession. His business. "A feeling of accomplishing something worthwhile."

Her intense green eyes challenged. "You think serving

food and giving others a delightful hour or so, entertaining them with pirate history is not worthwhile?"

His face heated. "Sure it is." He'd never have to explain this to his movie associates. "Entertaining just one person is important, but your talent could have a greater effect on hundreds, thousands—the world."

She gave him a studied look. "Is that what they're doing in those Hollywood films?"

Everyone here knew the answer to that.

"I see," he said.

Lizzie's parents had owned the Cave. It would be hers and Paul's now. Paul had a house at Tybee, and Lizzie had been raised there. She could live in the antebellum mansion, or a villa in Paris. What did she need with a part in a movie that could give her a chunk of money and fleeting fame, when she already had all the good things in life? She had no desire for what Hollywood had to offer.

He remembered that Symon had said *I see* when Lizzie told him she and Preston Bartholomew had talked about his book. They'd all known, and seen, that Zach had tried to access DeBerry through the back door.

It became quiet, as if someone had called for a moment of silence, so contemplation could take place, or prayer offered. If he were a praying man, he'd sure pray for wisdom, and the ability to refrain from saying another foolish thing. He bit off a chunk of brownie and smushed it in his mouth.

He'd tried to keep his eyes off Lizzie, but she was always there in his mind. That beautiful heart-shaped face, the slight tip of her head at times, making her bangs almost cover her eyebrows. Those gorgeous jewel-green eyes, that perfect nose and the luscious lips that had worn a smile the entire time at Tybee. Here, she seemed a mixture of confidence and vulnerability.

When she spoke, his eyes focused on her. It was as if she decided to come alive, in spite of his being there. He knew she held back that outgoing personality of hers. He'd seen it, basked in it, delighted in it—loved it?

"I do love acting," she said. "But I have no desire for Hollywood films. Most days I can hardly wait to get to the restaurant and become the pirate of the day."

The others laughed congenially. Her face became animated. Her eyes sparkled. He couldn't help but stare—she was actually speaking directly to him. He'd thought they were ignoring each other. Maybe it was only he who was doing the ignoring because he thought that's the way he needed to…act.

The others discussed the different roles Lizzie had played. They loved talking about it, too. So this conversation was for his benefit. He could hardly believe they could treat him so well, accept him, while knowing he'd misled Lizzie. Even Paul, but maybe that was because he knew Lizzie had no interest in Zach beyond cordiality.

Then she said the most astounding thing. "Symon said I'd make a great Red Lady in his movie. I did consider that." She wrinkled her nose at Symon and he grinned. "Then he had to go and turn down the offer."

"What?" Zach stared at Symon. "You…turned it down?" His astonishment increased when Symon quoted the amount of money offered for the rights to his book.

"I intend to keep control," Symon said. "After returning to Savannah, I committed my life to the Lord. He has to be in my work somewhere because He's in me. I insisted the production company include the moment of choice. They refused. They just want the blood and gore and evil. So I said no."

"Wowwww," Zach moaned.

Symon laughed. "I know how you feel. That's how I would have felt when I was climbing the ladder to success. I'd probably have done anything for a movie."

Zach's brow furrowed. "What choice do you mean?"

"I now include a moment when the killer thinks about his choice to kill or not. Anyone who has enough sense to plan a killing understands there are consequences and has sense enough to resist. I include that now so the reader thinks about it. In case a potential killer reads my books, either because of the lure of killing or to discover a vile new way to do it, he also reads the moment of choice."

Zach stared, thoughtful. "I know that's in *The Pirate's Treasure* and not in your others. I thought this was just a different kind of killer."

"No," Symon said. "It's a different kind of author."

Zach contemplated that for a moment. He needed to think like a producer. "That kind of information should be included in your video. The moment of choice. For a killer. And author."

Symon studied him and nodded. "I want it known that my identity is no longer bestselling novelist. It's being a child of God. A husband. A son to Aunt B. A friend. A mentor to other writers."

Zach understood. He was a Southern boy, had lived in the Bible Belt until age twelve. He'd been vaccinated, indoctrinated and it was inside himself somewhere.

Symon reached over and closed his hand over Annabelle's. "I'd rather return to being the caretaker in that cottage than miss out on what I now have—peace,' Annabelle, my mom—" his head indicated Miss B "—and my friends."

Zach couldn't pretend not to care about success. His discomfort must be showing.

"Just to be clear," Symon said. "I still want all the world can give. But more than that I want God's presence, His assurance, the promise of eternal life with Him. I'm still as human as ever, but I also have God's spirit and I choose to let the final decisions rest with Him."

"Scary, isn't it?" Zach said.

"Yes. But more scary not to." He smiled. "Makes me feel good."

Zach swallowed hard. Symon felt good about turning down the movie offer? "But you already have success."

Symon shrugged. "That can be transitory. Known today. Forgotten tomorrow."

Zach nodded. Yes, so true with actors. Fame could be short-lived. Too often fortune wasn't handled well, either. Great actors reduced to doing commercials to make ends meet.

"If I hadn't been successful I wouldn't have returned to Savannah to thank Aunt B for teaching me all those years when I was the caretaker's son," Symon explained. "God used success to bring me back. Usually people fail before realizing the need to depend on the Lord. So…" and he began explaining why he wanted a documentary about the arts. "I want to make a difference in the lives of aspiring writers, like Aunt B and many others did for me."

Zach agreed. "Your purpose and testimony needs to be emphasized. Your faith journey is more fascinating than the professional one."

"Exactly what I want known," he said, looking pleased. "I would like for you to make the documentary if it interests you." He lifted a hand. "No need to answer now. After Thanksgiving is what I had in mind. After the students return from their break. We have a lot of things going on before that. Besides teaching, I have another book deadline."

Zach thought a little honesty from him might help. "Thanks for the offer." He glanced around. "And I thank each of you for your openness. I'm not used to that."

"Takes practice," Aunt B said kindly.

"I acted like a clergyman," he said quickly, nervous. "But I'm really…the opposite." As if they didn't know. "You all are the real thing, aren't you?"

"Absolutely," Miss B said. "Not because we're good.

But we have committed our lives to the Lord. He's with us. And now that you've heard this you can't escape it. You can stifle it, reject it, refuse it, but you can't escape it."

"Thanks a lot," he joked.

"You're welcome," she said seriously.

Zach squirmed inside. He'd felt like a different person from the moment he returned to the South and fastened that collar around his neck. Sometimes it choked him. Everywhere he turned was a reminder of who he wasn't. As if God were trying to get him, or something.

The people in this house weren't acting. Their faith and behavior was real. He needed to get back to California and perspective.

His dad texted him immediately after seeing the awards show online. Later, he called, saying he and Carol wanted to hear all about it, and invited him to dinner.

Zach looked forward to it, and that night after they had finished eating, while Carol finished tidying up the kitchen, Zach and his dad settled in the den with coffee.

"I've been offered the lead role in *Loving Life,*" Zach said as he put his coffee on the table and sat in the recliner across from his dad. "I heard."

Zach had been sure his dad would jump up, embrace him and tell him how proud he was. He did none of that. Just looked at him and finally said, "It's supposed to be the most sensual role yet."

Zach nodded. "They're offering an enormous fee, and my agent says he can easily get more. I could be number one in the box office."

"Is that what you want?"

Truth? Maybe the openness he'd experienced down South had rubbed off on him, made him say, "I can't have what I want. I can have what I thought I wanted, but it's not what I want now. I want a girl who doesn't want me."

He went further and told his dad about his mistakes, how he had messed up his big opportunities.

A furrow appeared in his dad's brow, then he regarded Zach, serious. "I've taught you about moviemaking. Exposed you to it. Maybe opened a few doors for you. But I haven't done much in other ways. Personal or...faith."

Was his dad apologizing?

Zach grinned. "There was Christmas and Easter."

"Used to be," his dad said. "I was raised in the church. I know the remarks made about people who go to church only on those two occasions. As if we shouldn't be there. But those are the important days, Zach. The birth and resurrection of Jesus."

Zach couldn't believe his dad was talking like this. "Dad, you're a decent, good man."

His dad shook his head, and Zach wished the conversation would end. He didn't need to hear any secrets. "Am I?" Zach knew his dad was asking himself. "I'm decent in some areas because my second wife is a Christian woman. I'm faithful to her. I don't kill anybody, I don't curse at people, but I direct movies that often present those things as just the way life is."

"Isn't it?"

"Sometimes. But that's not all. It's easier to go along with glorifying wrong action and taking God's name in vain, instead of showing there are consequences and a better way. Carol recently subscribed to *Movieguide,* which features faith-based films with a moral. Makes me think."

Zach had seen some of the faith-based movies and thought most of them were poorly made.

Another thought intruded. If you can do it better, Zach...

Wham!

Where did that challenging thought come from?

Scary.

He focused on what his dad was saying. "Carol has brought to the forefront some things I'd pushed to the back of my mind. The way I used to live. What you accepted at Bible school when you were eleven years old."

Had he not just left the South and people who talked openly about themselves and their faith, he couldn't consider sharing with his dad. "You know why I did that?"

"I hope so, but your question makes me wonder."

"You and Mom had started arguing, not liking each other, and it seemed I couldn't do anything right, either. I felt as if you were starting not to care about me. If I could be a better boy, you'd like me better and like each other again."

His dad blew out a breath. "I don't know if I caused your mom to make her decisions. But I'm sorry I've ever hurt you."

"I'm a grown man, Dad."

His dad gave him a woeful look. "Nobody gets too grown to be hurt. But what I mean mainly is if I've hurt you from being the kind of person God intended you to be."

Zach could only stare, could not even blink, when his dad said, "I know you blame your mother." He paused as if this were as hard to say as it was for Zach to listen. But Zach had eaten a lot of humble pie recently and that overshadowed any award or movie offer.

"I put my acting ahead of your mother," his dad confessed. "That was my job, my dream, and I felt she should go along with it. Maybe it was my obsession." He sighed. "I don't know if I was right or wrong." He picked at a thread on his pants. "It wasn't just that. We had problems. The doctor was more like the kind of husband she wanted. And needed."

They sat in silence for a while and finally Zach asked, "Why are you telling me this now?"

His dad shrugged. "Maybe because you opened up to

me. Maybe because I remember I was just a little older than you when we moved to California. I didn't know all the answers. I've learned a few over the years. I didn't have anyone to vent to." He grinned. "I'm here for you to vent if you want."

Zach smiled and nodded.

"You have a big choice to make," his dad said.

Choice?

After he returned to his condo in Malibu, he couldn't stop thinking about Preston Bartholomew, a character, a role in a movie, who was the catalyst for showing him who he was, or wasn't. Preston had made him think seriously.

He almost laughed, thinking of his choice. He could choose taking the lead role in a box-office sure thing. And what would it bring him? Bigger house. More films. Fame. Money. Fans. Paparazzi. Women.

He would arrive.

He'd worked for this, had gotten to know people, won the awards. He was on his way up.

Up?

Where and what was up?

Okay, his other choice. Film a promo video any high school kid could film. Make a documentary for which he'd probably be paid a set fee, but not further his career.

What kind of choices were those?

He felt as if he were twelve again. Should he run and hide behind a tree? Chance taking a glass of punch to the hurt girl?

Scary?

Scary not to.

He lifted his face toward heaven. "Lord, I've been trying to make people and Hollywood and the world want me since I was twelve. I've messed up. I know You want me. You want what's left of me. Here I am. I'm...committing myself to You."

He remembered what Lizzie said she did after making a commitment. She promised God she'd break her date.

Maybe he should do something to prove his sincerity. No, that wasn't necessary. Or…was it? Miss B had said commitment is a daily journey.

He took a deep breath and released it. Then he punched the buttons on his phone.

After the conversation, which left his agent irate, Zach pocketed the phone. He had just ended his movie career.

Chapter 18

Lizzie threw away Smiling Jack and vowed she'd also throw out her ridiculous experience with Preston Bartholomew. She could no longer trust her ability to discern others, no matter how many people had complimented her for it in the past. She could no longer take pride in it. Obviously, she didn't have any discernment.

There! Done with that.

But it didn't mean she had to throw away her own smiles. She'd always been a lively, outgoing person and so she did what she set her mind to and counted her blessings throughout the Thanksgiving season.

The day after Thanksgiving dinner with her wonderful friends, including Aunt B's friend Clovis and her beau—both in their seventies! —who'd become quite lovey-dovey, Lizzie relished the excitement of the next holiday season, Christmas.

They dragged out all the decorations, including lights for the outside of Aunt B's house and the cottage. The guys brought in real trees. After all, they not only had the birth of Christ to celebrate but also the wedding of Aunt B and Henri.

While draping the white ribbon down the long curving banister of the staircase, Lizzie moaned, despite her resolve. "Aunt B is a friend and a mother to me." She sighed. "Now she's getting married before I do."

Annabelle cast her a sidelong glance. "Aren't mothers supposed to marry before their daughters?"

"Well…" Lizzie stood still, holding on to the roll of satin. "When you say it like that…"

They both burst into laughter.

She figured she'd be able to freely laugh about her escapade of falling for a character in about ten years or so, maybe to her nieces and nephews. Of course she would chalk this up as experience. She would never again take a person at his handsome-face value. So what if she often thought of Preston Bartholomew? He didn't exist.

Oddly, she also remembered Zachary Grant, and didn't object when Megan and Annabelle said they should check the movie news on TV. According to reports, Zach and Mario Victoro were still being considered for the part in *Loving Life*.

"I don't exactly respect that," Lizzie said. She'd never want to share her man that way.

"Well, he's not for you anyway, remember?" Annabelle teased. "What you've always wanted is a pirate."

Lizzie didn't refute that. She'd always dreamed of a pirate with a patch on his eye, a parrot on his shoulder, a crooked smile and a gleam in his eye as he said "Ahoy, matey" to sweep her up and carry her away.

"See?" Lizzie grimaced. "A real pirate doesn't exist, either. I'm a lost cause."

Their pitiful looks seemed to say they agreed with her.

She shook her head. "No more fantasy for me. Preston Bartholomew cured me."

"Right…" Annabelle and Megan said in unison.

Then Aunt B piped up. "You really think you could marry a clergyman?"

"No," she said honestly. "What appealed to me was the kind of faith he represented. I've always felt the man for me was out there and I'd know him when he appeared. The moment I saw Zach, I thought that was him. I was wrong." Her shoulders slumped.

"Frankly," Aunt B said, "I don't know how Zach stands a chance of not taking seriously his relationship with the Lord with all the things that are happening. None of this was coincidence, you know."

"I hope he does," Lizzie said. "But that has nothing to do with me and him. I related to Preston Bartholomew for a few days, not Zachary Grant. And it looks as if Zach might become an Adonis."

"And you don't think you both—" Annabelle began.

"Don't even go there," Lizzie said. "I've become realistic." To prove it, she clicked the TV's off button. "I thought we were going shopping."

They'd always loved going to the annual Christmas Made in the South event to buy unique gifts, even suggesting what they might get one another.

All afternoon Lizzie's mind remained on the arts and crafts as they trekked through the Convention Center, speaking with several of the hundreds of craftspeople and artists there to interact with shoppers.

"Look at these." Megan gestured to a tree decorated with one-of-a-kind ornaments that could be personalized.

Lizzie became intrigued by the glass-beaded jewelry. Annabelle wanted a tapestry for her holiday table.

Finally, laden with gifts and decorations, they sat down for specialty coffees. Annabelle's phone rang.

"Really?" she asked. "Well. Interesting. Okay. Love you. Bye."

Annabelle grinned.

"Are you going to say something or do we rip your tapestry?" Lizzie threatened.

"Looks as if we're having a guest for dinner tonight. Other than the usual Henri."

Lizzie spoke innocently. "I've been naughty and have to stay in my room tonight without supper."

Annabelle shook her head. "None of that. We're making progress with our seminar, Christmas and wedding plans. Can't do without you."

"Well, I can't do with meeting another man."

"Not another one," Annabelle said. "Same ole, same ole." She shrugged. "Just Zachary Grant."

Lizzie forced her jaw back in place, aware that she had been showing her tonsils.

Megan chuckled while Annabelle pointed to her phone. "Zach returned to the B and B and called Symon to say he'd film the video and documentary if he still wanted him."

"Then he didn't get the *Loving Life* role?"

"Symon said he did, but turned it down." Her eyes widened. "His agent is irate, and plans to drop him."

Lizzie figured the only reason he'd turn that down would be if he thought Symon might ask him to produce *The Pirate's Treasure*. Zach was taking a chance, but he'd done that...before.

No matter. He was here on business with Symon. She'd been cordial before. She could be again. Although she felt as though she'd be more comfortable holed up in one of the caves or tunnels.

When Zach arrived at Aunt B's, Symon immediately asked him why he turned down the movie lead.

Lizzie watched him take a deep breath as he addressed

Symon. "You all have made me think more about purpose and beyond the immediate project. My dad and I had a long discussion about his faith, about how he left it behind." He hugged himself. "I did that, too, when I was twelve." He stood tall. "My dad and I have decided to try and make a difference in Hollywood. Not accept that the audience wants sensual and violent content. We believe there's an audience that wants morality, integrity and a faith solution when possible."

He pointed at Symon. "That came from you. The kind of ingredient you want in your books."

Lizzie watched Symon's studied gaze at Zach. Maybe he, too, was wondering if this were real, or an act, or a ploy. Then Zach added, "Dad's wife suggested a book she's been reading. Thinks it would make an exciting movie, and it has the spiritual element included. He's looking into it."

Congratulatory remarks were made, and Willamina appeared in the doorway. "You finally getting some of that living water?" she said. "Humph. Anyway, y'all want this supper hot or cold?"

Everyone followed right behind her to the dining room. During supper, Zach mentioned that he was considering seeing his mom. "I'm working on…forgiveness."

"That came up before," Aunt B spoke kindly. "I believe you wanted to know why you should forgive if you still pay the consequences."

He frowned. "I might know, but I'd phrase it poorly. I'd like to hear your answer."

Lizzie admired the honesty with which Aunt B talked about her life. Everyone at the table had heard her story except Zach, but they never tired of hearing it. It was like a review of lessons in life and faith.

"I did not forgive my parents for many years," Aunt B said with a faraway look. "They made me give up my baby when I was sixteen. They rejected their own grandchild.

I harbored anger and bitterness, and when I finally tried to see it from their point of view, I began to see them as fallible human beings. Before that, they were perfect. My dad a senator. We lived in this big house, had everything, did everything. I even got to go to Paris. The city of romance. And I had my romance…at sixteen."

Lizzie saw Zach glance around as if he thought he might have asked for something too personal. Aunt B reached over and touched his hand in a comforting gesture, then returned her hand to her lap and continued, focusing mainly on Zach.

"In early years I thought I messed up my own life, and my parents' respect for me. I had this deep dark secret. But I had to forgive myself and my parents. That freed me from anger and bitterness. I took on a world of children and have been acclaimed as a revered teacher."

She glanced around the table. "My son died when he was eleven, and I now believe Henri, being a pediatrician, was the best parent for him. If I'd kept my baby, I wouldn't have taken Symon into my heart as my son. His and Annabelle's lives would be different. Now, I can say I'm truly glad for the good that has come. God can work in our lives, turn our messes into messages. I have His forgiveness, His peace, His joy."

Lizzie exchanged glances with her friends. Now Aunt B would marry the man who had adopted and raised her son. They were both his parents.

The natural turn of the conversation moved to plans for the wedding. Henri spoke up. "Zach, if you're going to be here for the wedding, maybe you could film it for us."

"If that's an invitation," he said and smiled broadly, "I accept. It would feel like coming full circle. When I was here twenty years ago, I was hurt and bitter. Maybe this time I could try and rid myself of that."

Aunt B smiled at him and nodded.

After dinner, Aunt B led them to the foyer where a beautifully decorated Christmas tree stood next to the staircase decorated with white satin ribbon. They discussed what she wanted filmed, and Zach made suggestions concerning lighting, background, and such.

Before she knew it, Lizzie's friends had scattered like they'd done after the other dinner they'd had here. She turned to leave the room.

Zach's words halted her. "Could I ask you something?"

"Sure." She had almost said no. It was hard to talk to him after what had happened between them.

"Can you forgive me?"

Lizzie had thought about that since the night she discovered he was not Preston Bartholomew, but an actor who had let a charade go too far. She looked at him and tried not to get lost in those appealing brown eyes. "Yes," she said simply.

Lizzie knew that Zach had been unable to forgive for twenty years. He needed friends and faith and healing more than he needed her. That's what she'd needed when her parents died so suddenly. Getting over loss didn't happen overnight.

She asked the pertinent question. "Can you forgive your mother?"

"I want to try." His gaze searched everywhere but her face, then finally settled on her eyes. "Will you go with me?"

"N-now?"

He grimaced. "I may not make it if I try alone."

Flashing through her mind was the idea that Symon, Noah, or Henri should go. But they had their spouses and fiancé.

She had time, and oddly the inclination also. And since she forgave him, she should ignore that niggling worrisome thing inside her and act…no, *behave* like an acquaintance who accepted him as her friends did.

She nodded. "All right."

"I rode here with Henri. Shall we take your car or should I borrow one?"

She quickly dismissed the urge to quip that they might borrow Symon's. After all, he wasn't Preston Bartholomew, he was Zachary Grant. And…which one had she forgiven?

Lizzie drove her car and he gave directions.

"I haven't admitted that I love my mother since I was twelve," Zach said as they neared his mother's house. "I've faced her with my obstinacy, my anger, my rejection."

"Do you really think your mom will reject you?" Lizzie asked.

He shook his head. "No, that's what bothers me."

They pulled into the driveway, and his mom must have heard the car, or been looking out the window, because the front door opened before he could ring the bell. There was so much to say. Two decades of explanation. Letting her know how he felt. How a boy reasons one way, a man another.

She peered past him. "Bring your girl in."

Zack turned and motioned. He couldn't find words for anything. But Lizzie walked up, introduced herself, and his mother invited them into the den.

She said to Lizzie, "This is my husband, Martin."

Martin turned off the TV, and Zach's mom moved a book from the couch to the end table. "Would you like to sit?"

He shook his head.

"I want to show you something," she said, and they followed her down the hall and into a bedroom. A bedroom that resembled the one he had when he was twelve, when his parents had lived together. The same posters. The pictures of him in all kinds of sports, things he'd never excelled in but enjoyed. Pictures of him with his mom and dad. Zach was puzzled. Dr. Scroff hadn't made her hide them or throw them out?

"I come in here and pray for you," she said, and he heard the catch in her voice.

She followed him and Lizzie back to the living room. Asked if they wanted tea or coffee. She had some great sweet rolls, too. Lizzie said, "No, thank you."

Zach's emotions shook his body. They both must see that. He would have run, but he glanced at Lizzie, and the encouragement he saw in her green eyes made him stay.

How to begin? Two decades of words. He opened his mouth and the words came. "I love you."

Before he could think, she was in his arms. "I know. I know." He saw the tears that soaked her face. Her body trembled as she laid her head against his chest. He thought his heart stopped beating. He couldn't breathe.

He saw Martin wipe a tear from his eye.

His mom reached up and touched Zach's face. "My boy."

"Forgive me?" he said.

"There was never anything to forgive. Can you forgive me?"

"I already have."

They released each other, and Zach walked over to Martin, who stood with an outstretched hand. Zach shook it. First time. He looked at his mom. "I need to go, but I'll be back."

She nodded. And smiled. That was his mom.

He turned to leave, and Lizzie was right beside him. Like a friend.

Yes, he'd be back. Free, this time. They didn't have to explain the past two decades. They could just start from… here.

Darkness had fallen, and he didn't start the car immediately. After a moment, he braced his arms over the steering wheel. "Actors chew a pill that makes their eyes water and their noses run. Others just remember the sad times of their lives and are able to cry." He scoffed lightly. "I know which category I'll fit into now."

Lizzie handed him a tissue.

"Thanks," he said after using it, and started the car.

"Could I ask you a question?" she said.

"Sure."

"How do you feel now?"

"Like I did when I turned down the role in *Loving Life.* Good."

She laughed lightly and smiled at him. "So do I."

Chapter 19

During the next week, each morning began with male time at the Fitness Center, female time in Miss B's basement and instead of separate devotion time, Zach gathered with them around Miss B's for a Willamina breakfast. Her threatening eyes seemed to have receded into only mild wariness toward him.

He ventured to say, "You're in this, too, you know."

With hands on her hips, she threatened, "You think you're going to turn me into a Hollywood movie star, you got another think coming."

"Don't you get those stars in your eyes now, Willamina. This is a Southern film."

She turned and poured a glass of water, then set it down in front of him. "You still need a good dose of this."

He chuckled, knowing she was again referring to that living water.

Willamina's fussing with him made him feel even more a part of the group. After breakfast, they had coffee while discussing the devotion, and Noah said his amazing prayers that hit the mark for each of their needs. It made Zach feel as if the Lord's arms were wrapped around him—in a way he'd missed from his mom over the past twenty years. Often, he had to squeeze his eyes just a little tighter to keep tears at bay, thinking of what he'd missed, and at the "Amen," he took a sip of water. Willamina was in the doorway, grinning.

"We need to get the documentary finished and out of the way," Symon said to the entire group, "so Zach can concentrate on filming the wedding." He looked at Zach. "How long can you stay in Savannah?"

"If we don't finish, I can return after the holidays." Becoming accustomed to their speaking so freely, he decided to try it. "I need to spend a little time getting reacquainted with my mom."

He looked at Lizzie and almost swallowed his tongue at the soft glow in her eyes and smile on her lips. He had to remind himself that wasn't for him, but the situation.

With difficulty, he looked away from her face and at Symon again. "I wouldn't mind making Savannah my home. Coming back to my roots."

Noah said, "Megan and I are talking about selling the B and B."

"Really?" Zach said. With some negotiation he might swing a down payment, use the upstairs as a B and B if needed and live on the main floor. "I love that place."

"Sorry," Megan said. "I'm afraid it's already spoken for."

"What?" Noah looked quickly at Megan, then followed her gaze to Lizzie, whose glance skittered toward Zach. "Well, I have to have someplace to live." She lifted a shoulder. "Nepotism."

Ah, she was adorable as she grinned at him. He forgot

about caution and said, "Maybe the new owner would consider renting out the second floor."

"Right." Obviously, Paul hadn't forgotten, as he jumped in on that one. "Maybe a few college girls, like when Annabelle, Megan and Lizzie lived there."

Paul treated him as a friend, but Zach felt his presence was always a warning: don't mess with my sister. Maybe he was referring to the fact that the B and B had strict rules about males and females fraternizing.

Lizzie actually laughed. "Producers come up with such great ideas, don't they?" It all seemed good-natured but the point was made that they were not together. At least they were kidding around, making innuendoes as if the possibility of a relationship between him and Lizzie *could* exist. But he was probably making too much of that.

It occurred to him, too, that when Lizzie said *nepotism* that decisions were often made because of who you knew. That's why he'd manipulated her to get to DeBerry. However, Lizzie getting first choice on the B and B wasn't a result of her misleading anyone, but because of friendship.

He'd like that to be the basis of a relationship with them all. Prove they could trust him. And he needed to prove that to himself. Zach attended church with them on Sunday, and they filled a pew. Henri, Miss B, Symon, Annabelle, Lizzie, Megan, Noah, Paul and him.

When it became time to film the doc, Zach had Dillon, a crew member, fly in to do the filming. Zach wanted to make this as professional as the California earthquake documentary.

For some strange reason…or was that some faith-based reason…he began to feel a sense of purpose in making a difference for others, not just in advancing his own career, although he had no objections to that, as Symon had said.

He loved the activity of the following days as he directed Dillon to capture the scenes at the university, in

Symon's home office and Miss B's dining room. His creative friends, with their varying talents and different backgrounds, were the perfect analogy to working together in the larger arena of media arts. Zach didn't know when he'd been more proud of a project.

The work went smoothly since he didn't have to do the usual shepherding of a production from start to finish. Symon's cast was a few college students and his friends. Everyone contributed to the script, which consisted of them revealing their own expertise, and how they worked together. Symon was financing the doc, so that was a huge burden out of the way. Zach's suggestion of the background music was approved. He edited, and the finished product was approved and applauded, as if he'd done it instead of the entire group. He suggested means of social media promotion.

Winning an award had no place in this. Winning the respect of these people who showed him what it was like to have faith, and live it and be a friend, became his purpose. Zach wanted their respect. He wanted Lizzie to think he was a decent guy, worthy of her friendship. It was still two weeks before Christmas and a week before the wedding, so Zach decided to throw out an idea of his own. "A documentary about the pirates who have frequented this area through the ages, primarily River Street, and of course the Pirate's Cave would be featured."

The way Symon stared at him made him think he might suspect Zach was still trying to weasel his way into his pirate book. Then the author said, "Fascinating subject." He laughed. "I did write a novel about it." His lips pursed thoughtfully. "You're welcome to use a scene from my book."

For an instant, Zach wondered if he should resist. Maybe this was a test. But no. He had a career. He had dreams and plans. He was an actor and a producer, even though he had no contracted project at the moment.

"That's certainly crossed my mind," he said, as a professional, not a conniver. "The Red Lady pirate scene. And of course the only one to play the part is the pirate lady herself." He glanced at Lizzie, whose green eyes were wide. She lifted her chin as if she might protest, so he hurried on, speaking to Symon. "Did you have anyone in mind for your hero?"

Symon shook his head. "I wasn't thinking about a movie when I wrote it. So nobody in particular. Just the kind of pirate who would appeal to the Red Lady, win her heart and tame her."

Zach couldn't win her heart. "She should not be tamed," he said. "She's the most alive, colorful, appealing woman—I mean, pirate in the world."

"Hmm," Symon said. "That's a great line for the script."

Zach thought he'd better not risk the ire of Lizzie or Paul. "That's just my observation as a producer."

Lizzie turned her face toward Megan and Annabelle, who sat across the table from her, and he was sure the women giggled.

Later, Zach talked with the men about something else that was on his mind. They, and even Paul, agreed to go along with it. Paul probably thought if Lizzie wanted to beat a fellow up, he wouldn't stop her this time, like he had when she was five years old.

Lizzie reminded herself Zach wasn't talking about her as the appealing woman, but simply as the character she played. Sort of like her seeing Preston Bartholomew instead of Zachary Grant.

She did think of protesting when he said he'd play the part of Captain Horatio Flint of the Seven Seas, but she reconsidered since she'd...forgiven him.

She wished she *had* protested when he appeared in a costume of boots, black-and-red-striped pants, a black vest with a huge silver buckle, a white blousy shirt with leather bands around the wrists and a black-and-red bandanna tied around his head. He had a sword in his hand and a patch over his eye.

With dimples in his cheeks and a wicked look flashing in his eye, he grinned as if he thought he might be able to tame the Red Lady after all.

Megan and Annabelle were the only ones who could come for the filming, besides Paul, who was already at the Cave, and Symon.

They warned Lizzie about going into the tunnels with Zach. "That's your fantasy," Annabelle said and Megan slowly nodded.

Lizzie scoffed. "That's a character."

"So was Preston Bartholomew."

"Exactly," Lizzie said. "That cured me."

They hummed.

But as they made their way down to the tunnel, she did say, as the Red Lady would to Captain Horatio Flint of the Seven Seas, "Just don't invade my space."

Amazing how just one dancing eye turned her way could speak volumes. Same with a flashing dimple. "That's what we need in this scene," he said. "The daring, courage and audaciousness of the lady." Well, he was in character. That's where she needed to get.

"I am an experienced pirate," she reminded him.

"But has she ever met Captain Horatio?"

"No matter," she scoffed. "As you have correctly observed, the Red Lady is daring, courageous and audacious." A nod punctuated that statement. And like a true pirate he grinned that enigmatic grin that made butterflies in her stomach flutter. Yes, she was in character.

As he gave instructions, much like what was written

in the book, they acted out a scene while Symon, Annabelle and Megan got as close as they could in the tunnels to watch.

Finally, Zach asked, "How's the audio?"

Dillon said, "We're good. It's a wrap."

The others turned and began to make their way out of the tunnels but Zach reached out and held her arm. "Look," he said. "I can't go on forever wondering if there's any chance for us. I can't stand being around you and pretending, acting as if I don't care."

She shook her head. "You tricked me, wearing that collar. You're not a clergyman."

He lifted his hands. His voice resonated through the tunnels. "So? You told me you were Veronica, the Red Lady. You wore a costume, a bandanna, spilled the yarn about being a pirate. You're not a pirate."

Her voice rose. "I play a part."

He barked, "So do I."

She shouted, "You should have told me right away."

"I had two reasons," he yelled. "One was to get to De-Berry." The harshness in his voice lessened. "The other was that I feared you wouldn't associate with me because you gave up dating. You made a vow. I didn't know what to do. I knew what I wanted to do from the moment I saw you."

Before she could even ask what he would have done, the swashbuckling pirate had her in his arms, his lips on hers, and the Red Lady became a trembling jellyfish. No spine. Then she was a woman, in the arms of a man she lo...lo...lov...oh, forget it, and she did, and it was impossible to think, just feel and enjoy.

He stood so close, his one eye staring at her with longing, his shoulders rising with deep breaths, which had nothing to do with limited air in a tunnel. It was limited air in the lungs. She knew, from experience.

And then her head was against his heart and his strong hand was in her hair at the back of her head. She'd been kissed by Preston Bartholomew and Captain Horatio Flint of the Seven Seas.

A voice broke into the scene. "What's going on down here?"

"I'm dead," Zach mumbled.

"What are you two doing? I heard yelling."

Lizzie looked over her shoulder and let go of her captain with only one hand. She waved at Paul as if he should go away. "We're staying in character. Just practicing."

Paul groaned and didn't kill Zach, just turned and walked away.

The Red Lady in her looked up at Captain Horatio. "I didn't know pirates wore cologne. I thought they smelled like rum and sweat."

He chuckled low. "I thought lady pirates washed their hair in sea water, if at all, not fragrant shampoo."

"Well," she teased. "A lady pirate can surprise you."

"Proceed," he said.

"And she can kiss as well as a buccaneer."

So she did. And if she hadn't been ridiculous enough already for loving Preston Bartholomew, she'd gone and fallen for Captain Horatio Flint of the Seven Seas.

He'd said he hadn't wanted to tame her. Too bad. That was his problem.

Finally, he asked, "Could we step into the cave?"

Since they were both pirates, and he'd tamed her *and* won her heart, she could only nod. He surprised her by going over to the treasure chest. "Something I wanted to see again." He lifted the lid and toyed around with the golden chains and coins, then bought out a miniature chest she'd never seen. Opening it, he said, "I believe this is yours."

She gasped and held her breath when she saw it. Then

her fingers gingerly lifted it from the chest, tears filling her eyes. A charm. The little silver heart with a rose etched inside.

"How…?" She leaned against the stone wall of the tunnel. "My mother gave this to me for my fifth birthday. When I discovered I had lost it, we searched and searched everywhere I'd been. I cried myself to sleep that night." She placed it in the palm of her hand then looked up at him. "Where did you get this?"

As he told her about that time twenty years ago, she remembered. It was the first wedding she'd ever been to. She thought the bride and groom had looked like a king and queen.

She hadn't really thought about getting married before. But she knew a lot about fairy tales, and she'd watched the boy who looked like a prince in one of the stories.

He was beautiful, but he didn't smile. A couple other boys had teased her about her freckles and red hair. She'd spilled punch on her new dress, the prettiest dress she ever had.

And she had gotten mad.

The one who made her spill her punch had said she had mud all over her face. That's when she'd tried to beat him up, but Paul had pulled her off and saved the boy.

She had gone inside to get cleaned up and when she returned, the beautiful boy had brought her a glass of punch. Paul had scared him away, though.

When I get married, she had said to Annabelle, *he's going to be nice.*

I'm not going to get married, Annabelle had replied. *I'm going to be a princess like Cinderella.*

Annabelle had grown up to be a queen, beauty queen to be precise. And then she married Symon, and they would live happily ever after.

Lizzie had felt like a princess that day until the meanie

had ruined it. Then she'd felt like a princess again with Preston Bartholomew, and thought Zach, the meanie, had ruined it.

Looking at him now acting like a pirate, she thought he *was* that beautiful boy.

She touched the charm in the palm of her hand, and looked up at him. "I lost my heart," she said. "And you had it all along."

He removed the patch from his eye, stepped closer and said low, "Am I invading your space?"

Breathless, she said, "I'll let you know."

She never did.

When they emerged topside, Zach engaged in conversation with Symon and Paul. Lizzie sat in a booth with Annabelle and Megan.

Megan said, before Lizzie could say anything, "We want to hear it all, but we've known it all along."

"Known what?"

"That you're in love, silly."

"Only with Preston," she denied, then added slowly, "And maybe the pirate." She told them about the charm. "And the beautiful boy."

Annabelle scoffed. "You've been an entirely different person. Before this you were the most…well, all those things Zach said about you, but you became completely discombobulated. We knew it was love." She lifted her hands. "We've been there, done that. In fact, we're in it."

Lizzie shrugged. "Well, we didn't make any lifelong plans. All we did was turn the underground into tunnels of love."

Was it love? She hadn't said it. But it sure was discombobulating. And they both seemed to love that, but there was a wedding underway, and it was the week before Christmas.

It was a small private gathering. Aunt B was elegant and beautiful at the top of the stairs, dressed in winter white with red accessories. Lizzie and their friends stood in the foyer, and when the music began, Aunt B descended the stairs and took the waiting hand of her handsome Parisian fiancé who was about to become her husband.

After the ceremony and a cake and punch reception in the dining room where Zach instructed Dillon about the pictures, Lizzie wandered down the hall and into the foyer where she glimpsed herself in the large gold-framed mirror.

She and her friends had given a lot of attention to detail on how they'd dress for Aunt B's wedding. She felt rather like a princess in the long black skirt with the flirty slit, topped with a chunky sequined knit top. She sparkled like Christmas, as she wandered into the living room to sit near the lighted tree.

She thought of outward appearances. Whether she was dressed for a wedding, a jean-clad figure riding a bike, a Red Lady in a pirate costume, a conservative girl at church, she was Lizzie. All her personalities, moods, characteristics, acting, being, were Lizzie.

And Preston Bartholomew, Captain Horatio Flint of the Seven Seas, the friend of her friends, the beautiful boy, were all Zachary Grant. She'd been pretending just like he had. Pretending that she wasn't in love with him. But the truth was, she had fallen in love with him at first glance when the wind blew him into the Pirate's Cave.

Seeing shiny black shoes topped by black pants, she gazed up to see the gorgeous actor, producer and friend dressed in a tuxedo with a red rose in his lapel.

"You look lonely," he said.

"Well, they all beat me to the altar." She shrugged and smiled. "Oh, well. Somebody has to be last."

"I've always heard the best of most things are saved 'til last."

She glanced toward the doorway. "Henri and Aunt B feel that way about each other. Now they're going to Israel."

"I'd like to say *'Ti amo, tantissima'* to my bride while on a honeymoon in Tuscany."

She was getting that funny feeling. "You have a bride?"

"I want one. I want you. I love you."

She grasped the edge of the seat. "Did Aunt B tell you about Tuscany?"

He grinned. "I had to ask someone for their blessing, didn't I?"

She was trying very hard to sit still and not become totally unhinged. "Who—who's speaking to me?"

"All my characters, and my heart and soul, love you. Only you."

"I love all of you, too."

"Will your characters marry my characters?"

"You could ask them. Let's see—" she touched her cheek with a delicate finger, coy "—I have about twenty-five pirate characters, maybe three dozen princesses and—"

He grasped her hand. "You," he said. "The total you. You see, the total me loves you…totally."

She nodded. "I've loved you for twenty years. Waited for you."

"I'm here. Forevermore. Will you marry me?"

"Yes."

He drew her up in front of him.

Applause sounded at the doorway. Then somebody began singing about it beginning to look a lot like Christmas.

Lizzie didn't look. She just felt his lips on hers and his arms around her waist. This was where she belonged.

She had a strong feeling that the one who had brought all this about, who knew their hearts, was that heavenly… seeking…Mr. Perfect.

* * * * *

REQUEST YOUR FREE BOOKS!

2 FREE INSPIRATIONAL NOVELS
PLUS 2
FREE
MYSTERY GIFTS

Love Inspired®

YES! Please send me 2 FREE Love Inspired® novels and my 2 FREE mystery gifts (gifts are worth about $10). After receiving them, if I don't wish to receive any more books, I can return the shipping statement marked "cancel." If I don't cancel, I will receive 6 brand-new novels every month and be billed just $4.74 per book in the U.S. or $5.24 per book in Canada. That's a savings of at least 21% off the cover price. It's quite a bargain! Shipping and handling is just 50¢ per book in the U.S. and 75¢ per book in Canada.* I understand that accepting the 2 free books and gifts places me under no obligation to buy anything. I can always return a shipment and cancel at any time. Even if I never buy another book, the two free books and gifts are mine to keep forever.

105/305 IDN F49N

Name _____ (PLEASE PRINT) _____

Address _____ Apt. # _____

City _____ State/Prov. _____ Zip/Postal Code _____

Signature (if under 18, a parent or guardian must sign) _____

Mail to the **Harlequin**® Reader Service:
IN U.S.A.: P.O. Box 1867, Buffalo, NY 14240-1867
IN CANADA: P.O. Box 609, Fort Erie, Ontario L2A 5X3

**Are you a subscriber to Love Inspired books
and want to receive the larger-print edition?
Call 1-800-873-8635 or visit www.ReaderService.com.**

* Terms and prices subject to change without notice. Prices do not include applicable taxes. Sales tax applicable in N.Y. Canadian residents will be charged applicable taxes. Offer not valid in Quebec. This offer is limited to one order per household. Not valid for current subscribers to Love Inspired books. All orders subject to credit approval. Credit or debit balances in a customer's account(s) may be offset by any other outstanding balance owed by or to the customer. Please allow 4 to 6 weeks for delivery. Offer available while quantities last.

Your Privacy—The Harlequin® Reader Service is committed to protecting your privacy. Our Privacy Policy is available online at www.ReaderService.com or upon request from the Harlequin Reader Service.
We make a portion of our mailing list available to reputable third parties that offer products we believe may interest you. If you prefer that we not exchange your name with third parties, or if you wish to clarify or modify your communication preferences, please visit us at www.ReaderService.com/consumerschoice or write to us at Harlequin Reader Service Preference Service, P.O. Box 9062, Buffalo, NY 14269. Include your complete name and address.

LIDIR13R

REQUEST YOUR FREE BOOKS!

2 FREE INSPIRATIONAL NOVELS
PLUS 2
FREE
MYSTERY GIFTS

Love Inspired.
HISTORICAL
INSPIRATIONAL HISTORICAL ROMANCE

YES! Please send me 2 FREE Love Inspired® Historical novels and my 2 FREE mystery gifts (gifts are worth about $10). After receiving them, if I don't wish to receive any more books, I can return the shipping statement marked "cancel." If I don't cancel, I will receive 4 brand-new novels every month and be billed just $4.74 per book in the U.S. or $5.24 per book in Canada. That's a savings of at least 21% off the cover price. It's quite a bargain! Shipping and handling is just 50¢ per book in the U.S. and 75¢ per book in Canada.* I understand that accepting the 2 free books and gifts places me under no obligation to buy anything. I can always return a shipment and cancel at any time. Even if I never buy another book, the two free books and gifts are mine to keep forever.

102/302 IDN F5CY

Name _____ (PLEASE PRINT) _____

Address _____ Apt. # _____

City _____ State/Prov. _____ Zip/Postal Code _____

Signature (if under 18, a parent or guardian must sign)

Mail to the **Harlequin® Reader Service:**
IN U.S.A.: P.O. Box 1867, Buffalo, NY 14240-1867
IN CANADA: P.O. Box 609, Fort Erie, Ontario L2A 5X3

Want to try two free books from another series?
Call 1-800-873-8635 or visit www.ReaderService.com.

* Terms and prices subject to change without notice. Prices do not include applicable taxes. Sales tax applicable in N.Y. Canadian residents will be charged applicable taxes. Offer not valid in Quebec. This offer is limited to one order per household. Not valid for current subscribers to Love Inspired Historical books. All orders subject to credit approval. Credit or debit balances in a customer's account(s) may be offset by any other outstanding balance owed by or to the customer. Please allow 4 to 6 weeks for delivery. Offer available while quantities last.

Your Privacy—The Harlequin® Reader Service is committed to protecting your privacy. Our Privacy Policy is available online at www.ReaderService.com or upon request from the Harlequin Reader Service.

We make a portion of our mailing list available to reputable third parties that offer products we believe may interest you. If you prefer that we not exchange your name with third parties, or if you wish to clarify or modify your communication preferences, please visit us at www.ReaderService.com/consumerschoice or write to us at Harlequin Reader Service Preference Service, P.O. Box 9062, Buffalo, NY 14269. Include your complete name and address.

LIHDIR13R

ReaderService.com

Manage your account online!

- Review your order history
- Manage your payments
- Update your address

*We've designed
the Harlequin® Reader Service
website just for you.*

Enjoy all the features!

- Reader excerpts from any series
- Respond to mailings and special monthly offers
- Discover new series available to you
- Browse the Bonus Bucks catalog
- Share your feedback

Visit us at:
ReaderService.com